Making Amends

Making Amends

by

Nisi Shawl

Seattle

Aqueduct Press

PO Box 95787

Seattle, Washington 98145-2787

www.aqueductpress.com

Library of Congress Control Number: 2024945152

ISBN: 978-1-61976-268-8

First Edition, January 2025

Cover Illustration by Luisah Teish

Book design by Kathryn Wilham

Acknowledgments

Heartfelt gratitude to the editors who first bought these stories, stories scattered and out of order and missing one another the way I know they did. Here they are together now, in large part thanks to you. I name those of you whose names I know: Nalo Hopkinson and Uppinder Mehan, Lesley Conner, John Joseph Adams, Rivqa Rafael and Tansy Rayner Roberts, Trevor Quachri, Athena Andreadis and Kay T. Holt, Josh Viola and Jason Heller, and Ursula Mayer. Of you all, Nalo gets the heartiest, feelingest gratitutde, as she supplied the inspiration behind "Out of the Black," and really the whole series, back in 2004.

Plus I owe special thanks to L. Timmel Duchamp, who proposed expanding that story into a booklength work of fiction. Your patience has been rewarded! And it only took 20 years!

I dedicate this book to the memory of my dear cousin, Vincent Troy Thompson, whom I last saw wearing chains and an orange jumpsuit.

Contents

Introduction

by Nalo Hopkinson

IN THE 1980S, when I was in my 20s and about 15 years away from being a writer, I set out to discover whether the only Black science fiction and fantasy authors in the genre were Samuel R. Delany (aka Chip), Tananarive Due, Charles Saunders, Octavia E. Butler, and Steven Barnes. This was in the years before personal computers and the Internet would change the way we searched for information. I had to do it the old-fashioned way; by using the library. Luckily, I worked for a public library system.

However, I also had to ferret out the information at a time when the popular (read: white) narrative in the science fiction and fantasy community about race was that it didn't matter, and the polite thing to do was not mention it; in effect, to cultivate a deliberate blindness to it. It was the time when even if you could get a science fiction and fantasy novel published that contained humans of color, chances were that the cover would show someone blue-skinned, or purple, or green; in fact, just about any other colour than the darker flesh tones and non-Caucasian features possessed by most of Earth's human inhabitants. It was well before Chip Delany's 1998 essay "Racism and Science Fiction" in the August issue of *The New York Review of Science Fiction* unequivocally called out the systemic racism in our community. So as I searched for Black writers in the field other than the big five, I had to become a detective, looking for hints and clues in story content, reviews, etc.

I found Claude-Michel Provost, a Haitian Canadian short story writer from Montreal who wrote in French. In English, years later, I discovered Nisi Shawl. They had recently had their first short story published in the April 1995 issue of *Asimov's Magazine*. The story title was "The Rainses." The public library came to the rescue again; I was eventually able to find and read a copy of Nisi's lovely ghost story. It had felt like a stretch for me to aspire to the status of the five Black anglophone novelists in the field. They had published many SF/F novels among them. But Nisi's existence, and their first short story publication in a professional SF/F magazine, let me know that SF/F publishing, though loathe to engage with the issue of representation at the time, might still let an emerging Black writer with obviously Black characters slip in here or there.

It was a few years more before I met Nisi; by then, we were both published authors. Though we come from different backgrounds—they are American and I am Caribbean—we found we had a lot in common. For instance, a similar love for and insistence on putting Black speech types on the page whenever we feel like it. A frank approach to sexuality in our writing. A love of cooking and herbalism. A resistance to body shaming, slut-shaming, enforced gender binarism. And so much more.

In 2004, Uppinder Mehan and I were editors of the fiction anthology *So Long Been Dreaming: Postcolonial Science Fiction*. Uppinder had conceived of it as an anthology of science fiction written by people of color. It may have been the first of its kind. Uppinder invited me to be his co-editor. We published Nisi's short story "Deep End" in that volume. "Deep End" is the original short story around which the stories in *Making Amends* are shaped.

I remember reading "Deep End" for the first time those many years ago. Nisi has the knack of planting the reader smack dab in the middle of the consequences of their science fiction premises, of deeply humanizing the people discounted and discarded by the conquest-driven state machine. Nisi creates living, breathing, laughing, loving, hating, eating, farting, fucking, grieving, breeding people, and for the space of reading the story, makes us live as those people, surviving in the world-machine, and sometimes, despite all the odds, thriving. Many authors can do that, but Nisi's particular spin on it is inimitable.

Let's start with that title: *Making Amends*. The doubling of meaning that Nisi crafts; a community of people convicted of crimes (I won't say "criminals," for reasons Nisi addresses in this collection) who have opted to take the sentence of settling an alien planet, which has been named "Amends." To save space and make the journey affordable, their original bodies are destroyed, and their consciousnesses stored then loaded at the other end of the journey into bodies cloned from those of their purported victims. The prisoners are given no choice over the race or sex of the bodies they're given.

Nisi's facility with the science-fictional jargon of space travel impresses me; how well they infuse it into the stew of frail human bodies, people finding love in dangerous places, the implacable unjustness of a justice system that treats humans as not just disposable, but literally as material.

Then there is Nisi's wordcraft, their ability to write prose that simultaneously possesses both economy and a vibrant liveliness: "*Robeson. Unique. Trill. Trill.*" The phrase consists only of the names of three of characters, uninflected on the face of it. But in a few short pages I'd already learned enough about Wayna, one of the protagonists of that story, that the simple line of names made my heart clench for her.

One of the pleasures of science fiction and fantasy for me, both as writer and reader, is its frequent practice of getting you to see the familiar in a different way. In *Making*

Amends, characters' sexualities are described with two terms I hadn't encountered before; that made me put the book down to think about them. Then I picked it back up right away because I wanted to know what the difficult, manipulative but very relatable protagonist was going to get up to next.

Nisi's sense of mischief is very much on display in this collection: take for instance their replacement of the phrase "pissed off" with "queefed off." That one made me laugh out loud, the substitution of a juicy new phrase which centers women's bodies.

Another sentence that made me give my brain a think, in the story "In Colors Everywhere," *"Odell wore no clothing, which meant Trill had no way of telling if the stranger was a him or a her."* The phrase neatly infers a wide swath of worldbuilding without halting the piece overlong with exposition.

I won't give away the ultimate final surprise of the piece; actually, there are two. Suffice to say, they expand the possibilities of the world of *Making Amends* into spaces I didn't anticipate. I love that. Speaking of which...

Love. This is the overwhelming feeling I come away with from reading these assembled stories. Love of humanity. Love of the inadvertent outliers who strive to be themselves. To make community. To live. It's not all rainbows and syllabub. In fact, that may be the smaller part of what goes on. There is illness and death, manipulation and murder. But at the end, a deep, lovely sweetness. *Making Amends* is a gift, as is all Nisi Shawl's writing.

My Recipe for Making Amends

STARTING AN INTERSTELLAR penal colony could be an extremely practical idea, right? It could even provide a sponsoring corporation a good Return on Investment — though of course the initial investment would be massive. *Making Amends* is my series of short stories about a corporate government trying to put this idea into action, and then about the idea's lovely and unforeseen consequences.

The first installment of the Making Amends series to appear was "Out of the Black," then titled "Deep End." In 2003, Nalo Hopkinson asked me to send her an anti-colonial science fiction story for her 2004 anthology *So Long Been Dreaming*, and my mind kept turning to historical examples of how empires had spread themselves. Australia, a long-running success, began as an extension of Britain's prisons, a dumping ground for debtors, revolutionaries, and other undesirables. I took that as my model: let convicts face the unknown dangers of life on alien worlds, the hostile animals, poisonous plants, and whatever other weirdnesses a strange ecosystem threw their way. If they were injured or died, well, too bad, but after all, these were criminals and not a great loss — though the benefits they won, such as mineral rights, would of course belong to the supervising political and financial entities.

There's an obvious problem with extrapolating the Australian set-up into space, and that's the prohibitive expense of hauling the necessary mass across the distance between Earth and any other at least semi-habitable planet. I solved that by stripping the transported prisoners of their flesh. Downloading and uploading consciousness is a familiar science fictional concept. I made it more appropriately cruel by describing it as a very painful process, part of the punishment.

Conceiving of these convicts as strings of data stored on a rocket-borne computer made them a lighter load, which made the whole venture much more feasible, economically speaking. Plus, it meant I didn't have to worry about calculating the stresses human freight would be subject to during acceleration and deceleration. No bodies, no stress. And it also solved the problem of how long they'd have to spend aboard their interstellar rocket ship: if the prisoners were reduced to mere software programs, they could be run slowly, or intermittently shut down. So, at sub-light speeds these expeditions to other stars would take decades, centuries even — but not according to the prisoners' perceptions. For them, the time would be long and tedious, but not necessarily interminable, unless those in control preferred to make that their prisoners' experience by ramping up the software's run-time.

The final fillip of whatthefuckery I added to "Out of the Black's" premise was to stipulate that the bodies into which the convicts' consciousness would be downloaded were cloned from the genetic material of their supposed "victims." Thus a doctor providing abortions could be reborn into a body copied from the DNA of an aborted fetus, or a strike organizer into one copied from a corporation's CEO.

"Out of the Black" raised lots of questions, but despite Aqueduct publisher L. Timmel Duchamp's invitation to expand it into a novel, I didn't feel the immediate need to answer them. Eventually I wrote seven other stories that supposedly do that, though they probably raise others. They appear here in the chronological order of the stories' events, rather than in the order I wrote and published them, which I hope makes them make more sense.

Much of what goes on in the series resurfaces more than once. The question of control kept coming up as I wrote these stories, for instance. The creation of an autonomous second AI meant that the original first AI, responsible for implementing the decisions of a fascist regime, had to give up control of its creation's operations. The narrator of "Out of the Black," Wayna, is subject to uncontrollable pain, and in "Out of the Black" and the later stories, prisoners are subjected to the control of the colony's trustees, and through those trustees, the control of the state that exiled them.

Another common thread is the mutability of antagonism and the blurring of lines of enmity. The AI in charge of the Amends mission could well be taken to be the enemy of the prisoners, especially when they try to win their autonomy, but his position is more nuanced, and subject to change. For the first generation of Amends settlers, the connection between their consciousness and their flesh is potentially a hostile one. Trustees are put in positions of power that make them enemies of their fellow prisoners despite their shared concerns. And always the environments through which my stories' characters move must be adapted to, placated, integrated into their lives. There are the stultifying class hierarchies embedded in the Earth-orbiting habitat where "Best Friend" takes place, the hard vacuum surrounding the mission's spaceships in "Over a Long Time Ago" and "Out of the Black," and of course, the alien landscape of Amends itself. All these tensions are explored, in all their ramifications.

By the time we see Jubilee, which is the Amends settlement at the center of these stories, the prisoners brought there have begun naming elements of their surroundings. Glow-in-the-dark Chrismas trees and Hannakka bushes soften the nights. Multicolored Rosetoos bloom and fruit, cured redvines bind the walls of their homes and accessorize their clothing, and they fish the waters of Unrest Bay and scavenge the eggs prettybirds lay in the Rainshadow Mountains.

One question I've faced from some editors and reviewers when talking about this series and a few other stories I've written is: What did my imprisoned characters do wrong, and what justifies their treatment?

The short answer, the answer I give once I've quieted my fury enough to respond coherently is: "Nothing." Nothing justifies the police persecution experienced by the hero of "Lazzrus" and "Sunshine of Your Love;" nothing excuses the confinement and exile of the involuntary inhabitants of Amends.

The longer, more specific answer I give tallies up behaviors recently re-problematized: seeking and providing abortions, presentation as an unassigned gender, non-heteronormative sexual interactions, and so on.

My home community is the African diaspora in the United States, specifically in Kalamazoo, Michigan. In my neighborhood there was never a need to discuss *why* someone was incarcerated. Incarceration was axiomatic, a basic condition of our lives. This past is the root of my resistance to the question. And the unfurling bud at the tip of the tree of my resistance is my dawning realization that I and many others—maybe you yourself—could easily be classified as criminals. Indeed, many of us are classified that way already.

In *Making Amends* I do my best to describe the steps and ingredients needed for us to break out of that oppressive categorization and into the deliciously wild unknown.

The Best Friend We Never Had

JOSIE STARED HARD at the woman standing just outside the connecting hose's exit. The expandable tubing she walked through was well-insulated, but for most of its length dimmer even than her ship had been. Still, though the light bleeding in from the exit to Mizar 5's concourse dazzled Josie's eyes, this woman's face looked unexpectedly familiar. Not the wig, though.

She kept staring as she walked. Was it going to be this easy to get in touch with the people she wanted to recruit? With Yale? Every step down the hose's gradient made Josie heavier and more certain who was waiting for her: obviously fake eyebrows slanting dramatically toward the shallow-bridged nose; hairline a perfect half-oval; smooth, ultra-medium brown skin — no, faint lines marked the former smoothness. She could see that now. And yet — "Lucky?"

Lucky's smile grew core bright. "You recognize me! Yeah, when I saw who was comin and it would be on my hours I told Twilla and Blaise and them you wouldn't forget."

"Course not." Though maybe she remembered the good old days differently. Saw them differently now, the fights and sickbay and jailtime. The friendships. The betrayal.

"How long you back for? For good?"

Josie had paused to talk to Lucky though she didn't really need a greeter; the hab's web had synched while her ship approached. Directions to her keep blinked in the window above her visual field. She could have followed them right off. But this would help her mission.

"Vacation," she said. The simplest truth. She'd be working, too, of course. No need to tell Lucky yet.

Lucky's mouth stayed in the same position, but her forehead moved up. "You'll hafta be away from there for years. ARPA gives vacations that long?"

Josie nodded. "Project's in a dormant phase." Till she recruited a crew for the starship they were developing. Six or seven "volunteers" who didn't mind leaving their bodies behind. Which she was convinced would be better for them than what would happen to her school otherwise. "I have to be back in time for the next big push." At least this way they'd be trustees rather than regular prisoners.

Relaxing her forehead, Lucky squinched her smiling mouth into make-believe disgust. "And you can't say what exactly it is you doin, cause ARPA."

"Yeah." The silence after her one-word answer filled with awkwardness. "Well—"

"Look." Lucky held out a tiny silver tab. An unofficial interface to private data—when Josie left Mizar 5 only residents on the shorter yet more lucrative Able and Bitch work-shifts could afford them, and they'd been subdural, but she'd read in the latest version that you only had to keep steadily in touch with—

"Your hair nappy enough it'll stay if you tuck it in."

Josie had quit wigs out there. "What's on it?"

"Contacts for me and the rest of our old school. And like that. If you wanna get together sometime, set it up?"

Josie took the tab, slipped it into position so it could interact with her skin's biome and the routines embedded below.

"All right!" Lucky nodded, slick orange curls bobbing below her drooping earlobes. "And you synched up so you know where your keep is, yeah? Catch you later, then."

So simple. She could lure them in all at once, an entire crew. Worth a pile of shares. And monitoring their journey to Amends as assigned would be a total piece of carb.

Josie crossed the concourse to join a clump of Able-monogrammed shoppers. She let herself be towed along spinward with them till her directions flashed for her to let go of the rope. Her keep was part of a complex organized around a noodle place. Ables lolled in a couple of padded niches, sipping frothy drinks and slurping bowls of fragrant soup. A pair of impatient-eyed Crowns waited to clear them out: it was almost 25 o'clock, time for shift change. Time for Crowns to play.

A sleepy-faced Bitch leaned into the armpit of one of the Ables. People did cross work shifts for pleasure, but they paid for it. Not only in confused circadians. Fights between shifts broke the endless routine, so of course they happened, with and without warning, which led to the sort of accusations Maree had faced one time. No one liked a traitor.

Ostracism. That was the worst. Consequences for fights didn't matter half as much. Sickbay was just more boredom. Expensive, though. But jail was a joke. Or it used to be; not so much the new facility.

Josie's directions pointed her to a set of plastic boards projecting out from the furthest-in wall. They formed steep stairs. No big deal, even in the hab's higher gravity. The ship's gym had been minimal, but there hadn't been too much to do on the way in besides train. Same basic routine as at the ARPA outpost.

There were a protective rail and a series of grips spaced along the wall above the boards. She ignored them and skipped every other step, waving at the Crowns below, who appeared to check their interfaces and ID her. Evidently. Thanks, gov. They stopped looking up as she hit the second-from-the-last riser, turning their attention back to the lingering Ables.

An opening at the top of the stairs became a corridor lined with four tall hatches. One hung wide. Directions claimed this was it. Josie stepped over the high sill and shut the hatch behind her, noting automatically the soft shush of meeting seals. The walls were pale turquoise, freshly coated. Floor and scuffguards lavender, same as the controls and handles for the closets, water and dry. Josie lowered the bedsit, revealing a mirrored ceiling. She pulled out the desk so it shelved over her knees as she sat, opened it up. Another mirror. The previous occupant had had some quirks. Josie didn't expect she'd be here long enough that they'd annoy her.

She sang a measure of her security code and the desk booted, showing the bland wallpaper she'd chosen, a few harmless-appearing icons. Her mission wasn't exactly a secret, but ARPA preferred a low profile. Subversives didn't need to know how far along they were with the project.

Satisfied, she set the desk to project a jazz score. Next, a shower. Josie stripped off her robe and tights. The robe would do for later—not the newest style, but she hadn't worn it enough to stink it up. The tights, though, were fab stock. She kicked them under the bedsit to get them out of her way and squeezed into the already running water closet. And out again fast.

The silver tab from Lucky hadn't gotten very wet. Maybe it didn't matter? She laid it on the desk anyway and went back in the water. Scrubbing absently at her strong shoulders, slat-ribbed sides, hips, legs—too bad they weren't longer—she puzzled briefly over why unofficial private interfaces had become popular. Something to do with escaping attention? Might subversives be involved? Because of gov everyone on Mizar 5, however high or low their shares, had plenty of storage and computing and communication capacity. Could be nothing more than a fad. Whatever Able and Bitch wanted they got. Then Crown picked up the leftovers and copied the two richer shifts.

Hard to soap between her toes in the tiny WC; like on the ship she had to lift her knees to her chin to reach them, but those were some of the best external spots to raise her personal biome's microbes. She wanted them well fed.

She turned the water off, got out wet because she'd forgotten to order new tights fabbed, got back in again, and turned on the heater and fan. By the time she'd dried off, the order was hanging from the fab frame in the other closet.

She strapped up and dressed. Baldric, holster, tights, and robe, though she was tired and longed for bed. Crown shift had seven more hours awake. Seven more hours for Josie's first shot at recruiting. She needed to align her circadians with that. She retrieved the silver tab from the desk to slip it in her hair — stopped.

No longer silver. She rolled the flattened cylinder in her pink palm. Now it gleamed black and blue.

Had that little bit of water…what was the word? Tarnished it? So quickly? Unlikely.

Nothing she'd seen before she headed out to ARPA, nothing she'd learned on the way back in, would explain this.

Josie was not putting some strangely mutated interface anywhere near her head. Those were her slickest routines up there. She set it carefully on the desk.

Fine. She had researched the school enough before she arrived. Should be easy to find her old friends even without Lucky's help.

Yes. Here were the notes she'd transferred from the ship's memory: addresses for keeps, protocols for messages, share statuses as of the most recent market, current employment — which last wouldn't do her any good till sixteen o'clock. Fifteen hours, almost. Too long. ARPA didn't class recruiting Crowns as a priority; she'd have to go for Ables and Bitches first if she couldn't reach the others in her old school right away.

Which was why she felt guilty switching off the projection and signing into Binocc. Almost no one used the site anymore, but Yale still had a page, and Josie had formed the habit of visiting it during the lonely voyage home. A stupid, pointless pleasure; he'd made his allegiance to Maree clear well before Josie responded to ARPA's offer. The very qualities that made her attractive to ARPA — her competitiveness, her skepticism, her lack of trust — had driven him away from her and into Maree's soft, soothing arms. Those two were lifers, judging by how they clung together.

The Binocc page predated Maree and didn't much mention her besides noting Yale's "Partnered" status. Josie scanned it. Nothing any different. Clips of his music, contest swag, stills and runs of him spitting verses, his wide green eyes focused on distant listeners. Round, dimpled cheeks belying his slender build — she remembered back in cresh when he'd been so chubby and determined not to be left behind by her and the other fast runners. But now —

Now she was wasting time. She checked her clock. A little before two. Crowns would be heading out from their keeps. Question was, where to?

Not here. She'd find them a lot faster if she headed out herself. Anywhere she figured she needed to get she could ask her field directions.

At the hatch she hesitated, went back to the desk for Lucky's tab, slipped it in her robe's bottom hem pocket. It couldn't hurt her from there. Maybe while poking around she'd learn what had caused the alarming color change.

Down the steps. Now Bitches leaned on their elbows behind the shop's counter. No customers. Ables should be asleep by this time. Crowns weren't big spenders. Wherever her school was hanging would be cheap.

The tow took her past massage parlors, churches, drops for fab stock. Then she saw a likely spot: a theater. She let go. Her school had always had a thing for live action.

The marquee told her the name of the production: Expanded Metal. Music. Yale's name wasn't on the bill. No one else she recognized, either. She bought a ticket anyway on a hunch. ARPA was good for it, and if the theater didn't pan out she'd plan her next move from here.

The seating area seemed sparsely filled. Out of a hundred seats, over half stayed empty as the lights dimmed. The act began and Josie understood why. Greasy-looking twinks, bare-topped and wearing kilts sewn together out of plaid patches, swung at each other with chrome-colored sticks. When the sticks connected, sounds — chimes clanging, hollow bangs, and rhythmic screeches — emerged from speakers arranged in the area's walls and ceiling. The program loaded to her field informed her she could listen internally instead.

There was a third option. Josie stood and edged past her row's only other occupant. The nearest hatch led to a different corridor than the one she'd entered by, and that led to the back access. And her school.

Oleanders bristled out of the access's walls from shoulder height up, filtering the droning, flickering lamps above. In the half-dark she recognized Hammer, Blaise, Vixi, Twilla, Lucky, and Lukie, the son born right before Josie left — everyone. Except where was Yale?

The tops of the bushes to her left rustled, loud and harsh. Josie looked over as a giggling, pink-faced drunk peered through their foliage. Oh, right. Maree. She'd totally forgotten her.

That only made Yale's absence weirder.

"Climb down before you scratch and poison yourself!" Lucky was always the school's mother, at it long before Lukie's birth.

"Climb down!" the young squirt echoed her. He'd be his school's mother, too.

"Don't wanna get caught!" Maree yelled.

"Then shut the fucks up!" Vixi never cared who she queefed off.

Burping and hiccupping, Yale's wife disentangled herself from the oleander branches and fell to the access's grated floor. Lucky hauled her upright, glancing at Josie. "Glad you could come—ain't been the same since you took off."

Right about then was when everyone's permanent work assignments went to fulltime, that was all. Left less energy to enjoy fights. Nothing to do with whether she was there.

Maree leaned against the wall, hunching her shoulders to avoid the bushes. "Josie? Josie come home? Too bad, girl. Too—" Like a whip snapping, Maree's spine flexed. A slug of vomit leaked between her lips, but she appeared to swallow most of it.

Josie turned away. Blaise grinned, gold teeth winking brighter as the hatch Josie had closed behind her opened. One of the twinks from the show stepped out. "You may wanna think to quiet down a shade," she said, shutting it again. "Intermission. Audience will hear you plain."

Lucky nodded. "We about to head off anyhow in a couple. Sure you can't join us?" She laid a hand against the musician's sweat-gleaming upper arm like it was a hatch control.

"Sure you can't stay for the gig?"

"You compin the entire school?"

The twink shook her head no. "Only you; the rest have to pay like—"

"I need to pee!" Maree complained. She tugged at Lucky's shoulder veil; with a shrug of annoyance, Lucky shook it off. "Come ON! Tab said we'd be there by four!"

Vixi ducked to retrieve the veil. "She has a point."

Lucky tilted her head back till her chin pointed at the white flowers dangling off the highest pipes. Her throat quivered, then seemed to freeze solid. Her jaw unclenched. "Don't *matter*! We can change what the tab cache *say*!"

"Yeah, but I NEED TO PEE!"

The hatch opened again, a sliver of crimson blocked by the twink musician's twisting body. An apologetic "I gotta go on," and she untwisted and vanished. The closing crack shifted to emerald green before it, too, vanished.

"Well, then." Lucky didn't sound as disappointed as Josie knew she must be. "Let's set it up." She looked at Josie as if for confirmation. Why? Josie gave a half-nod, not sure what she was agreeing with.

Then they were stomping down the access to a ramp, a ladder down further, a bridge over roaring ducts far, far below, barely visible. Josie had a good idea where they were headed: corewards. To a location they'd always managed to reach despite gov's attempts to block them: Mizar 5's forbidden center. Directions in her field agreed.

Sure enough, they halted halfway across the bridge. "Who first?" asked Lucky.

Once a repair crew had turned the local gravity bar back on, supposedly accidentally. Massive injuries for Lucky and Vixi that night. Sickbay massive.

All eyes on Josie. As if in a dream she pushed at the fence enclosing the walkway, finding the inevitable slit. It was in a different place than she remembered, and the cuts were fresh, the plastic sharp-edged where it had been sheared off. She threw one leg over the handrail. The other. Balanced. Fell. Fast. Faster. Her robe fluttered like the petals of a furious flower.

Fast but not far: soon she slowed. Slo-o-o-owed. Till she could snag a handle protruding from one of the hatches in the giant ducts now surrounding her and hover, waiting.

When the school had drifted into formation around her she pushed off from her duct and swam without hesitation for the nursery pod, the bulbous chamber where the hab's oxy-generating vegetation grew from seed to sprout to transplantable shrub.

The hatch in wouldn't open. A thick red cuff encircled and obscured its controls. Vixi tapped on Josie's arm to get her to move aside and rubbed a tab over them—as silver as Josie's had been originally. The cuff sprang apart, exposing the controls' edges. Now they worked. Now she pulled, and the hatch swung out.

Shining like a hundred suns, the nursery lights poured brilliance upon brilliance onto the oleanders' leathery leaves. They burned at 360 degrees of almost every circle that could be imagined, leaving nothing in shadow. Nothing hidden. Five other hatches showed in the sphere's curving wall, blank and bright. Ziggurats of hydroponic caskets stuck out from it in gradually higher rows, peaks and valleys of dark green. On the top of every towering stack a fan was mounted. On the bottom, where Maree was intent on getting fast, bright-capped fluid intakes.

Otherwise the nursery was empty. Josie realized she'd expected to find Yale here. This was where he used to spend his volunteer work shifts before his permanent assignment, where he would come to find peace, to meditate when upset by gov's too-transparent maneuverings. Despite how the oleanders' toxicity underlined its distrust, how gov had chosen a poisonous oxy generator on the theory non-poisonous ones would be eaten, Yale admired every variety of the species in every way. He should have been a botanist, not an ice harvester.

He should have been here.

She looked at Lucky. "Where is he?"

"Who?"

Josie just kept looking.

The smooth parts of Lucky's face got smoother. The dents deepened. "Thought you knew. Gone."

Gone? Deported? "How?"

"Shares run low—he kept sendin em down to Earth to his parents till it was only subsistence level left." No one wanted to live on subsistence. And eventually—

Mizar 5 had power, food, water, and air enough for everyone brought up or born here. Like that mattered. Use up your shares and you got thrown back in the dirt. Ables and Bitches especially hated "freeloading" Crowns, only allowed up from Earth because they'd won a lottery. Or rather because their parents had.

"Gov sent him down?" If she'd gotten here in time she could have—sort of—saved him from that.

"They was fixin—What now?"

Maree let go of Lucky's veil to fist tears from her cheeks. Pulling up her tights with the other hand. "You ain't gotta tell her. Let me. I was his wife. You take care of business."

Was. So much for being a lifer.

"Yeah, you right. Go ahead, then."

Lucky swooped off toward where Hammer and Blaise tossed Lukie back and forth between tower tops. "Tenshun! Time to get ready. We ain't *that* early!"

Maree side-eyed her. Josie grabbed a casket edge and adjusted her position so they were on the same plane.

"You never liked me, didja Josie?"

"No." Why lie?

Lukie started crying. Josie rotated slightly to see what was wrong. Lucky had him by his tights, wedging him under a fan housing.

"But Yale always talked about you and how best of a friend you was, so even if it makes me so sad I can't—even if it breaks" my *heart*—" Glistening with snot, Maree's pink nose flared. "—I'ma make myself tell you how he died."

Wait. "How he—*died?*" No reason for that—Mizar 5 medicine was as good as anything ARPA had. Which was the best.

But it took shares to buy it.

"He didn't wanna be sent down." Sniff. "I was gonna tell him I changed my mind to go with him. I was!"

Josie felt stupid—maybe due to lack of sleep. "What—what—"

"I didn't want his fucksin life insurance! Let every Bitch and Able we ever beat have it! I only wanted hi-i-i-im!" Wailing now. She still hadn't told Josie how—if Josie didn't hear—

He'd still be dead. For the first time since she could, since her ship synched with Mizar 5, Josie let herself query Yale's location. Last known was sickbay. Eight hundred shifts ago, as a transfer from the newly built General Holding. Diagnosis: cancer. Etiology: radiation exposure. Chance of recovery sans medication: zero.

Didn't make any sense.

Josie pushed herself away from the sobbing Maree. Why bother crying? She aimed for Lucky, but a softly smiling Hammer intercepted her. "Lucky says if you rather just watch, you prolly fit where that fan there mounted. We can take it down fast if you like."

She had to be getting stupider. "Watch what?"

Hammer's bald head drew back. "The fight. With the Bitches—you came cause of the invitation, right?" She must have looked as stupid as she felt. "The invitation Lucky gave you? One the tab accessed?"

The tab—she dug it out of her robe's hem pocket. "This?"

Hammer flinched away from it—from her. "When did it start lookin that way?"

"I—uh—I had it in my hair when I got in the shower. Could that—"

"No." Hammer shook his head so hard his whole body moved to counterbalance it. "What we got here is a reaction to your biome's tracking tech." They had a way to find that out?

Hammer flipped away. "Lucky! Our girl's wearin a wire."

"Say again?" Lucky took a big shiny purple ball from her loudly protesting squirt's hand. "You see how them fools at the cresh gave him a candyball? He coulda choked—"

Four of the six hatches opened at the same time. In dived angry Bitches. Robeless and roaring, they swarmed towards the free space at the nursery's center.

"Strip and strike!" Lucky yelled, hurling the candyball at the closest Bitch's head. Hitting his temple. He spasmed, and the line behind him stalled a moment to avoid his flailing limbs. The others kept coming, though. Aiming at her? Get your opponents off balance. Josie tore free of her robe and slung it at their faces. All that did was ram her back into the fan. The cloth sailed harmlessly past her targets.

But at least now she could reach her weapon. She dragged her sting from the baldric's back holster, whipped it at the black-browed Bitch lunging at her. Wrapped the tip around the Bitch's naked arm. Squeezed the switch.

The Bitch gasped for breath. Couldn't get enough. The sting's cardiac glycosides prevented that. Josie waited a count of three to disengage, momentarily ignoring the blows of the two Bitches prying at her weapon's grip. Used its butt to jab back at the one behind her and her open hand to hook the neckline of the one in front. Recoil from the jab bashed her head against his chin. Surprise! A come hither flick-and-jerk of the sting brought a third into their circle. Discharge. Release with a whirl that twirled her to face the one recovering from the punch to his belly. And a loop around his waist, but of course his tights impeded her sting's poison. She tossed him into the stunned chin-casualty's wide-open arms. And release.

This was the dance. So good with the proper equipment.

A lash to the second Bitch's still-dazed face caught him on the eyelids. He'd go under fast now. Josie didn't have to count. She did anyway, for fun. A new Bitch was on her before she finished, one who'd evidently fought a few rounds in low grav. But not against Josie. Not against Josie with an ARPA-issue sting.

The Bitch shoved off from a sheet-topped casket. Josie appreciated the counter-clockwise spin she added, obviously designed to negate the sting's wrap. Granted Josie was right-dominant. But when she got tired of stalking Yale on the trip in, she'd had nothing to do but come up with new ways to practice. She swapped the sting to her left and aimed for the Bitch's bare feet. When she had control of those, poison flooding through the Bitch's skin, Josie yanked hard. Beautiful! They began orbiting around an axis that wobbled lightly to the beat of the Bitch's twitching attempts to climb the sting. To choke her. Josie let the Bitch get close enough to touch her throat before losing consciousness. Safe, she kissed the Bitch on both her plump cheeks.

Safe. No more attackers. Among her Crowns only Maree obviously injured, one arm cradled in the other with its hand tucked in the crook of her elbow. Outnumbered two to one, her school had chewed the fourteen Bitches up: broken their bones, trapped them with nets and bolos, strangled them to the point of unconsciousness. Add to that her poisoning. If any moved, they were floating gently to the walls. Josie joined in with the work of towing them to the hatch her school had come in by.

"We gonna leave em here or try and take em to sickbay?" asked Twilla.

Hammer eyed Josie suspiciously. "Bet we don't got long to wait till sickbay come to us."

"Why?" asked Lucky. "You was sayin somethin before we stepped into it about a wire?"

A nod in Josie's direction. "The tab you gave her turned. Looks like she did, too."

Lucky grinned. "Well, fucks. Tell me somethin I didn't already figure out for myself."

Twilla frowned. "You work for ARPA, though, doncha, Jo?"

She wasn't supposed to know they'd tagged her biome for tracking. But it was a pretty obvious move; even Lucky had expected it.

"If you're so smart why'd you give a tab to her in the —"

"Who you think ARPA *is*, Twilla? They used to be DARPA, and that 'D' stood for defense. Like military. Like gov. Yeah." Bending over a snoring Bitch, Lucky straightened out an awkwardly angled thigh. "Josie's employer ain't no secret, and if she agreed to come along with us tonight it's obvious nothin we did was gonna be a surprise. In fact, havin somebody outta ARPA around probably what kept us from gettin hauled off to jail."

Of course that was when the drones came. Gassed everyone.

❦

Josie regained consciousness in the dark. No feed — her field glared stark white against the surrounding black. Pressure on her back; felt like she lay in full Mizar 5 gravity. She listened a while for more clues to where she was.

The echo of her breath came back almost instantly from nearby walls. A soft, barely detectable breeze swept past her ears. It carried the scent of — oleanders, certainly, but on top of that?

Depressants of some sort: she was obviously in jail again. Why? That wasn't part of the deal. How could she convince her school that a trip to Amends was a smart alternative if she was incarcerated too?

She must have done something wrong. Useless to struggle…

The depressants. With a snort she forced herself to sit. Which triggered the cell's lights and camera. A blue recording signal winked on to the left of the waist-to-head-high hatch.

Fabric covered most of her skin. Confirming this was legit gov: public, not some private porno channel.

"What's the charges? When do I get counsel?" She aimed her questions at the camera lens, assuming a mic somewhere in its vicinity.

A voice issued from the bed she lay on. "If you wish to replenish or excrete fluids you may use the facilities beneath you."

She stood. Not too wobbly. Repeated her questions. No answer.

The bed's base was a water cupboard. This was a fancier cell than the ones she'd wound up in before hiring on at ARPA. In the new facilities? She'd get out soon as she could.

"Thanks," she said. To whom or what? She drank from the cupboard's tap and squatted over its pot. The camera's light stayed on, but probably it couldn't record everything she did inside the cupboard. If she had to stay here long enough —

The hatch lifted. Lifted but didn't open, since all the retraction of the cover did was reveal a metal screen. Someone Josie couldn't completely see was walking toward her. A few steps and he became visible through the screen's gaps. A man. A white man. A smiling white man with long dark bangs, wearing a robe that glimmered like far-off lamps. "Josie." No point in him asking. It was a simple statement.

"Who're you?"

"Your counsel. ARPA's paying me to get you off the riot and battery." Like they wouldn't have been able to keep her out of here without all that legal stuff.

But her head was getting clearer. The depressants had triggered ARPA's drug immunity implant. If ARPA was paying to get her off, they still needed her for something.

"My name's Berbarian," the man added.

"Like the singer?"

Through the metal, Berbarian looked shocked. "How—" He stopped himself, but Josie knew what he had been about to say.

"Crown cresh has as much access to data banks as Bitch or Able." Anybody could know just about anything.

And like that, she was queefed. Royally. Not just because she was stuck teaching Shiftism 101 again. Because Yale was dead. Dead. Lucky and all the rest of her so-called friends had known—for how long? And no one had told her.

Not that she'd asked. But they could have told her. Could have said something.

"Crown's what you call C shift. Right." Berbarian glanced at something she couldn't see below the hatch frame. "So. Do you want to accept my services and acknowledge the sovereignty—I mean, the—" He checked himself. "—sovereignty which will give ARPA the right to claim you temporarily from Mizar 5 juris—"

"'Temporarily'?" ARPA had to have known about Yale. They hadn't told her either. Had no doubt filtered her stalking of him on the trip in.

"Yes. Long enough, don't worry. They'll get you in the buyout, anyway, but that could take a while." Her blank expression must have given him the courage to continue. "It's not exactly a take-over; they're forming a new political corporation, actually, with some of the old Earth-based contractors. Pick up additional freight."

Freight equaled subversives. Prisoners.

"Who? Who's forming a corporation?"

"ARPA."

Another thing they hadn't told her. Well, and why should they?

Josie stood still a moment, then turned away from the hatch. The cell was small. She paced it five times before Berbarian spoke again. "So you'll authorize me to request your release in my custody?"

What *had* ARPA told her? Anything true?

What about her mission? Did they in fact need to recruit six crewmembers to fly the starship they were building? Was she going to be able to sign her school up before they did something that classified them as subversives? And then supervise them remotely—

"If you don't authorize me you'll have to wait here in general population holding till the contracts take effect."

Judging from this one, the new general holding units stunk same as the old. Not all the oleanders stuffed in their walls would help. Plus because of their location along Mizar 5's hull, radiation storms hit them worse. People jailed here got ill first and treated last. If they even had the necessary shares to buy a cure. As Yale must have understood.

Who'd sent him here? Did he refuse deportation?

Yale used to sing to the plants as he set their pots in the hab walls' grooves. Said it made them grow better.

Angry tears hurt her eyes. She ducked her head into the cupboard and sipped more water as an excuse. She had to calm down. The tears fell, and then her eyes felt better for a moment. The only good that did. There was paper under there. She blew her nose and wiped her face.

Get the opponent off balance—and keep them there. Everybody was Josie's opponent until proven otherwise. What wouldn't Berbarian expect from her?

"Did they pick a name?"

"A—"

She stood up as straight as she could. Her legs were too short. Yale hadn't cared. Had laughed when she complained, called her his "hoppagrass." Whatever that meant.

"For the corporation. Or are they going to hold a contest like they did to name Mizar 5?"

"They—In the docs we've drawn up so far, it's called WestHem. I fail to see what the name's got to do with your decision." He clutched his bangs one-handed and gathered them in the middle of his forehead. "If you could focus on that for a moment—" His other hand appeared above the hatch frame. It held a handdesk. A big one, filling most of his square palm. "—I've got an agreement template here you can accept as is or modify."

Nudging her back to the script. She tried an oblique line of departure. Betting he didn't know what she would be talking about she asked, "How's my mission covered in there?"

Fucks. He didn't exactly smirk, but his hair-tugging hand dropped and his eyelids lowered and relaxed. Like he'd gotten something he wanted. "A release for that's included. Since the first phase of the original assignment is now unnecessary."

"Show me!" Josie realized she'd pressed herself against the screen and stepped back. Now who was off balance?

The handdesk's window displayed text. She read about the roster getting filled with "volunteers from the ranks of the recently fined and incarcerated." She could imagine Maree, Vixi—all of them except Lucky, probably, would have signed up rather than serve a lengthy sentence in holding. Maybe even Lucky, if they'd take Lukie on the starship too. That would fill the roster.

More or less what she had been aiming for. She settled her weight on her heels. But ARPA wanted something besides that. Something her signature would give them. Wanted Josie to accept counsel so she could get out of here and head back to the heliopause intact, moving on to her assignment's next phase: a century plugged into life-extension and hibernation tech, making sure the starship's crew and cargo reached Amends. Coaching them. Training them to be the penal colony's trustees.

Which was going to be harder to do if her school thought she'd betrayed them. At least Lucky had never doubted her. But if she left here in her body like no one else was going to—

"So?"

"Okay." Giving way was bound to be unexpected. "But I'll need a couple revisions."

↢

It made sense for ARPA-WestHem to site its first disassembly station here on Mizar 5. Why spend months shipping bodies out to the heliopause? They were only going to be left behind. And if the space they'd built here was larger than it needed to be, the blame could be laid on the hab's engineers' disinclination to lopsidedness. They'd solved a similar problem when constructing the new general holding facilities by wrapping the cells around the hab's equator. Matching the disassembly station's mass to the newly constructed immigrant processing center 180 degrees away meant it was huge, as if over a dozen keeps had been strung end-to-end, then doubled back on themselves.

Of course that brought up the question of where all those immigrants would go once they were processed. Josie hadn't envied Lucky the task of explaining to Lukie why half the hab was closing down. The noodle shop below the keep she'd left was vacant, taped off like the rest of that complex. Like a bunch of others.

Lucky had made her bargain, bought her way out of holding with the shares Josie gave her, deliberately vague about what she was paying her for. Nothing, really. Faith. Josie had made her bargain, too, and she wouldn't be around when it became obvious to the squirt what was happening with all the incoming prisoners. Let Lucky worry about explaining that. Josie would be out of reach, would soon after be light years gone.

Five hatches. She walked in through the third in the row, stepped carefully down the steep stairs on the far side. The disassembly station's grooved walls were still bare of plants. The air smelled burnt without them. Sealant fumes, coating volatiles, freed particles from cut metals and plastics, each added their distinctive aromas.

Stacks of freshly fabbed materials lined her path across the floor. On the far side they formed a high enough wall she had to walk around it to see the waiting chairs and soundproof vaults.

All four chairs were out. And empty. But used—they smelled like cleanser. Fine. Josie hadn't expected to go first. Run times would determine the order in which they became conscious.

Lucky walked into view around the side of the furthest vault. She looked back over her shoulder. Lukie emerged following her. "Careful now." He carried a lacy-shelled data block about the size of his head. Standard. Was everything that made her Josie supposed to fit on that? And should a *child* be allowed to handle it?

"Now where you gonna leave it?" Lucky asked.

"Here."

"Naw, that's the chair I'm plannin to sit Ms. Josie in. Cause the track drives right into this." She indicated an open-hatched vault. "How about the next one?"

Lukie ignored his mother's instructions and kept trudging along the line of chairs. He hefted his burden onto the cushioned recliner directly in front of Josie. "Are you having a good shift, Ms. Josie?" So formal. So serious. How much did he know?

"I'm doin," she replied. "Who's—what's on this?"

"Blank," Lucky assured her. "He wants to help, and I had to find somethin for him to fuss over."

Quickly, before she could think about it, Josie went to the seat nearest Lucky and sat. Then she got back up and removed her robe. "Will my tights make any difference?"

"Not according to how I been taught." They both eyed the Crowns attaching tiles to the upper wall. "Keep em on and they get destroyed when the scanners kick in, or take em off and I'll add em to fab stock after I shut down."

Destroyed. Like her whole body. She'd already donated samples from which to grow the clone her mind would, presumably, be downloaded into once Amends was reached. Goodbye everything else.

Including Lucky—who knew what Josie had tried to do, maybe even why, and hadn't tried to stop her.

She sat again. No sense stalling. Let Lucky strap her in. To be talking, she asked about the others from their old school. If they'd been surprised at the offer. If they'd said anything about her, whether they trusted her or believed she was behind things. If they'd thought to ask for any special conditions. Yes, no, none.

Not even Maree had asked for what Josie wanted. What she'd been positive she'd get in exchange for taking Lucky's spot, for supervising onsite rather than remotely.

Yale.

Not Yale. But near enough. His body. Someone else's mind but his body, cultured from research samples.

His body. Maybe his heart. His soul. Who could say where those were?

Lucky brushed back a stray lock of orange and looked down at her. "Ready? It's only gonna hurt a little while." No drugs. Full, unaltered consciousness was necessary for a viable record. When her last nerve was torn apart there'd be no more pain. Nothing to feel. A dreamless sleep.

Till she woke.

Over a Long Time Ago

SHE SHOULD GO back inside the watchpod. Maree and Blaise didn't have to be dead. The air hadn't been gone that long. And even if their current bodies were hopeless, damaged beyond repair, probably the back-up system was uncorrupted. Probably its uploads of those two—as well as the uploads of all the other prisoners—were just fine. Josie could confirm that, then crawl into her cryo drawer. Shut herself down.

But she stayed outside, watching the stars.

The stars were strange. They weren't the constellations Josie had grown up with on her home habitat, Mizar 5, and not even the marginally familiar ones she'd seen when stationed back at the heliopause, working for ARPA. They burned in new configurations that shifted against the black emptiness in dreamlike drifts: far and farther, past and to come. Untwinkling. Uninvolved.

"Come on." She said it out loud. She'd started off talking to Yale's body—*her* body—like that when she first woke up on the ship inside of his skin. *Her* skin. Her blood, her bones. Her balls and dik.

"Come on," she repeated. She made herself turn away from the spectacle of space and face the blown hatch. It had banged wide open in explosive but silent decompression sometime after she EVAed in an irritated huff. How long ago? A dimly shining cloud of frozen moisture was still visible in the ship's wake.

At the speed *Deliverer* traveled, roughly a tenth of light, that cloud of ejected air was eventually going to be left behind. Like Josie would have been if not for the umbilical line tying her to the watchpod and *Deliverer's* temporarily disabled oxygen supply. Whatever blew the hatch had tripped her suit's ventilation over to internal reserves, which were capacious and even semi-self-renewing. But she shouldn't count on them. She should go in and investigate the trouble. Maybe it was so simple she'd be able to deal with it herself. Sighing, she took hold of the umble with mittened hands and began hauling herself toward the hatchway.

No lights inside the airlock or watchpod. No glowing emergency strips. Nothing but darkness. Nothing but her memory of the layout to guide her. And the layout might have changed because of whatever had happened, so she chinned her helmet's torch on. There lay Blaise, right in front of her, sprawled on his side on the control couch, with Maree kneeling over him. His pale nakedness was glazed with ice—probably sweat. Straps kept both of them tethered to the couch. Maree's annoyingly long hair—defiantly, she'd let it grow for the six years since Josie downloaded her—stood out from her head in multiple directions like iron files on a magnet, exposing her red, ruined face. Just as well a length of cloth swaddled Blaise's.

Josie looked up from the dead lovers. Up. Centrifugrav still worked. A soft push, and the arch of the watchpod's ceiling was easy to reach. All-systems manual override was a mechanical switch. She flipped it, and *Deliverer's* emergency isolated electricals came online. Soothing blue lights shimmered around the vents and the spreadscreens.

But the screens stayed blank. Maybe reset was going to take a while? And replenishing the atmosphere would take a while, too; her suit's ventilation hadn't gone back on the umbilical's feed yet. Plus, why had *Deliverer's* atmosphere vanished in the first place?

Priorities. On the primitive glass display panel, all 2543 prisoner flags showed as green, including her own. So, good.

The uploads were intact. The prisoners' instances were safe. The power link for the stasis chamber in the storage pod opposite this one looked good, and given all the ship's failsafes, Josie was relatively sure the tissues the prisoners' bodies were going to be cloned from would also be fine. The mission was salvageable.

Blaise's ice coating had melted. Progress. But best remove his recorder before things warmed up any further. When she took off her suit he'd be smelly. Might as well get Maree's recorder too. Selecting a scalpel from the medical kit hooked to the couch, she peeled back the cloth covering Blaise's face — a repurposed modesty skirt, it looked like, ironically — clenched her teeth, and began slicing. Though the mess was much worse than it ought to have been, his nose was pretty much intact.

Maree was messier. Josie had to resort to digging through a pulpy mound of snot and blood and meat and hair to find the camera that had been embedded at her nose's tip. Which was a drag, especially in mittens. Nasty, awkward work. And lonely.

She wiped everything off with the clean part of the modesty skirt and snapped the first camera into her helmet's port, set to play. Skipped ahead to today, 04032064. The images filling her heads-up stuttered. That was normal; frame capture rate on these things was intentionally slow. Only enough exposures per minute to pick out highlights that a back-up instance of the downloaded prisoner might need to incorporate.

She'd zipped past the flirting, which hadn't been as subtle as either of her old schoolmates believed. Josie hated being left out. But when Maree learned that Josie had chosen to download Maree in order to fuck her with Yale's body, that sort of soured the relationship. Maybe Josie shouldn't have pretended to be Yale. Not even for just a few moments. Downloading Blaise, too — ostensibly because his pro-tech tendencies enhanced the ship-operating engrams ARPA gave everyone — had defused tensions for a while. Then....

There she went on the playback, suited up and shoulder-ing between Blaise's viewpoint and Maree's heaving shoulders. The camera followed the Yale/Josie image to the lock, then jerked back to Maree before the lock's controls registered being touched. After several vigorous close-ups and zoom-outs, the run went white. Then it stopped.

Switching to Maree's camera, she saw a similar sequence. The Josie interruption came with a smear of red along the picture's bottom, signal of some negative emotion on Maree's part—guilt or hate, probably, or both. The emotional smudge passed swiftly as Maree turned back to her sex partner. Her camera captured her hands landing a number of slaps to Blaise's plump cheeks. White fabric crumpled up and swished around in the playback's foreground as the skirt was tied in place. All of a sudden the skirt fluttered madly, billowed out, and collapsed. And the recording was over. Wait—an alpha-numeric flashed up briefly and was gone. Too fast to read.

Apparently the decompression had happened near-ly instantaneously. Most likely caused by a micrometeoroid, though *Deliverer* was hundreds of thousands of AU from any planetary system. The whipple shield should have caught any stray particles, anyway. But what else could it be? A microme-teoroid. That was the only remotely reasonable possibility.

She ran through the end of the second sequence again. The alphanumeric flash was gone. And it stayed gone when she ran it four more times.

Giving up, she followed procedure, unleashing the crawlers to find and plug any holes. Now nothing detained her from collecting Blaise and Maree's corpses and bundling them into the shredder. They fit, but it took multiple flushes to clear the line of their slurry.

She tried to pretend there was nothing grisly about what she was doing. To focus on retrieving the raw materials crucial for growing her old schoolmates' new bodies. Waste not, want not.

Afterwards, there was plenty of room in the watchpod. Too much room, actually. Which prisoner should she bring back? Who would make the most tractable trustee? An updated instance of Maree would treat Josie with the same chilliness this last one had exhibited since discovering Josie's plot to score revenge sex on her. So probably not Maree. But not Blaise either; he was decidedly non-mirror bias, and had obviously considered sexing with Yale's body a distasteful duty. Twilla? No; she *was* mirror bias. Deeply. She'd be more put off by Yale's body than Blaise had been. Vixi?

The crawlers were visible to Josie's unaided eyes as a multicolored sheen stretching along the join between the pod's control wall and its narrow floor. Such a large concentration suggested they'd found their work. They were replicating themselves; next, they'd either transport or copy whatever materials they needed to patch whatever holes they'd found.

With a few more swipes she got rid of the last of the fluids clinging to the couch and settled down to wait for the return to normalcy. The suit felt so isolating. She'd have to ask Vixi for a massage. Or maybe she should promote and download someone she didn't know from her old school, some other promising prisoner pulled from the storage banks.

Leaning back, Josie docked her helmet into the couch's outlet to scan the prisoner list. Her heads-up sprang to life but showed only an empty blue oblong. No icon. No menu. No scrollbar.

She lifted her head and disengaged. Re-docked. Still nothing but the oblong.

Had the micrometeroid crash triggered a processor reset? But redundancies should have prevented a complete wipe of the system. Josie counted the seconds to verify that a problem had actually occurred: one thousand, two thousand…twenty thousand, and no change.

She tried voice activation. No reaction.

What about her private system's link-up? That had been part of the deal she struck with ARPA when she agreed to take Lucky's place on *Deliverer*—installation of her chips and antennae in Yale's body, complete with a dedicated communication channel. She'd used those extras only a few times.

Anxiously, she hummed the summoning sequence and success! Her home room opened in its dedicated corner of her visual field. She hadn't spent a lot of thought on furnishing it—no thought at all, in fact. So it retained its presets: peach-colored walls, white ceiling, beige carpet, scattered tables and plant stands, and a single couch covered in white-and-green stripes.

Another hum and a smiling avatar greeted her—the algorithms Josie had selected to operate her system, bundled together in a glossier, longer-legged-version of her original embodiment. ARPA's finest tech.

"How's it hangin?" she asked the avatar.

"Here and now? All good." One of the standard responses she'd configured it for.

"Good. Get me a current list of our prisoners, uh, I mean clients."

"The loading manifest? Sure."

"So the list hasn't changed since we launched?" The project's directors had warned of possible data degradation due to radiation sneaking past the computer core's shields. It was a vanishingly small possibility, but it was a real one. Not imaginary. "What's the manifest's most recent version?"

"I can't retrieve that."

"Of course you can. Talk to *Deliverer*."

"Not getting through."

"What? Why not?" If the watchpod's rudimentary display panel could link to *Deliverer's* computer core, Josie's softa personal system should have zero problems making the same connection. In fact—

"Piggyback on the display panel's line."

"I tried. It's discontinuous."

The line was discontinuous. The line between the watchpod and *Deliverer's* computer core was broken. That made no sense.

"Then how is the display getting data?"

"It isn't."

"But it is!" She kept her audio on but ducked out of the home room to look at the panel again. "See?" Ducked back.

"When disrupted, the display reverts to showing its last available data."

"That's a really stupid idea."

The avatar shrugged. "If you say so." Another standard response.

"And what's going on with the—the clients? How are we—how am I supposed to know? They're my responsibility!"

What good did it do to shout at herself? She shut off the audio and left.

There was an emergency computer access port on *Deliverer's* core. To get there she'd have to EVA. Again. But at least she still had on the suit. Which must stink by now. Could she at least catch a breath of fresh air before going out?

Mitten on her neck zipper, Josie hesitated. She sat up— too easily. She stood. Also too easily. Centrifugrav felt weaker now than when she'd come in from EVA, which was the exact opposite of how things ought to be tending. So what about the atmosphere? Was there any? Was it getting thicker? Had enough been siphoned from the reserves in the storage pod on the *Deliverer's* far side? According to the suit's sensors everything should be fine—but what if it wasn't?

She unzipped herself a bare finger's width and heard through vacuum-muffled ears the bright whistle of escaping gas. Rezipped fast as she could.

The patch of crawlers lay motionless, all the same color: matte green. That meant they were done with their job. The hole or holes must be fixed. No more leaking. No more air going out. Therefore, the issue had to be that no air was coming in. Shuffling carefully forward, Josie stuck her hand on the duct outlet and felt no movement. No pressure.

All right then. Core ho. She stopped by the airlock to unhook the umble and strap on a wrist lamp. The lock's mechanical gauge confirmed the watchpod's airlessness. She closed the hatches tight behind her anyway.

Something was wrong with the stars. Clinging to the hatch's handle, Josie stopped to stare at them a moment. Were they…not moving? Hard to tell this far from anything she recognized.

She aimed a beam from her wrist lamp aft. She had to sweep her arm back and forth a bit before the light caught on the shimmering water crystals expelled by the watchpod's decompression. Shouldn't they be—lower? Further south? She ought to review the engrams.

The arm and conduits connecting the watchpod to *Deliverer's* central module were affixed to the side opposite the airlock. Josie tapped her wrist light twice so it would stay on and started pulling herself over the pod's exterior by its built-in holds. When she came to the connecting arm she hugged it; it was too thick around for her hands to meet, but WestHem's training said to use her embrace to move herself inward. It worked. Hunch slide hunch slide hunch slide hunch slide….

She needed to pause and rest. A few times, despite her dedication to exercising on *Deliverer's* elliptical. This used another set of muscle groups. During the second-to-last stop she tried shining her light to the left to catch one of the struts anchoring the ship's sail. She couldn't see it.

Because it wasn't there.

She checked the engram with *Deliverer's* blueprints that ARPA had embedded in her brain. Yes, the light sail's struts ought to rise off the ship's core a few more hunches forward. But though Josie played her wrist light in ever-widening arcs, it kept showing her nothing.

Horror shrank her skin tight and cold. Maintaining her calm — for whose good? Must be for her own — she twisted to throw the light's beam the other direction. And *there* was a strut, right where one was supposed to be. Following it outward, her wrist light's thin beam gave her a glimpse of a stark white cylinder branching into the ribs supporting that part of the sail. So something was fine. Staring in that direction, she thought she caught a couple of stars appearing, emerging from behind the laser-shot sail that powered *Deliverer's* interstellar flight. Then a golden wisp edged into view: a nebula. The vast blot of the sail's silhouette no longer blocked it.

But these emergences were slow — too slow. The nebula and stars had come into view with *Deliverer's* progress as a whole. They weren't happening because of the watchpod's arm whirling properly around the core, because the arm wasn't whirling properly. Which she should have known because the strut was practically staying still. Like the arm she climbed.

No wonder centrifugrav had all but vanished. And that was what was wrong with the stars. And the frozen cloud of air. That was what had been bothering her. The stars weren't behaving. They weren't going around in fast-enough circles.

Wrongness upon wrongness.

Were there invisible connections between these disasters? The blown atmosphere, the system wipe, the suit readouts, the negligible spin, the missing strut…. Sabotage? But by who? Nobody else was aboard besides her fellow prisoners, and *Deliverer* had strong safeguards preventing their escape and embodiment.

That didn't matter to the building dread threatening to swallow her heart and mind.

Work was one of Josie's favorite ways to stifle mindless fear. But she didn't have the engrams for assessing and repairing damage this widespread. She was going to have to access someone else's upload. All the more reason to get into *Deliverer's* core module and tell whoever could handle this exactly what was happening. She started forward again. Only a short ways to go.

A survey of the core's surface as it rotated lazily past showed three of the sail's four support struts in place. Josie stepped cautiously from the ring halfheartedly propelling the watchpod's arm and finished her EVA at the core's hatch. She wrestled the hatch open and wondered what she would have done if the other struts had been gone too. Wondered what should be done about that missing fourth one. Though really that wasn't her job.

She was a manager. She recruited and assigned and coached. A people person. She clung to that definition of herself. Her job was to find someone to fix things. She would do it.

"On," she told the core unit's life support. It came up without a hitch. Illumination. Ventilation, too—but she needed to keep the suit on to dock. Might as well stay sealed.

In many ways the interior of *Deliverer's* core made Josie think of the greenhouse at the center of Mizar 5. There were the glowing light fixtures dotting its curved walls and the tangled vines climbing its terraces; there was that same feeling of floating—but the core's smaller scale reminded her that Earth and its habitats were a lightmonth behind them. And that Yale, who she used to believe would always be safe in that sheltered spot, was long gone from there. From everywhere. Only a duplicate of his body existed anymore, and only here, and only because she had insisted on it.

She hauled herself over to the computer access port. This time when she docked, her heads-up showed a normal page, dark grey alphanumeric on a pale green ground. She was about to select the option for searching client bios when a rapid fluttering started in the corner of her vision dedicated to her private system. An alert! Josie'd never gotten one before—her system was fairly passive.

Dutifully, she hummed. Her avatar sprang up like a hopeless crush. "Don't touch anything!" Frantically, the avatar waved its slender, Josie-modeled hands. "De-dock! There's a virus—I'm fighting it off but it's weird and I don't can't while you if hurrying to stop what goes? What? No, makes and seems! No yes?"

Josie jerked free of the dock. "That better?"

The avatar nodded. Its puffy hair bounced realistically. "Thank you!"

Should she stay disengaged till *Deliverer* repelled the attack? So much else was already going on. She had to do *something*. How could the avatar help? "Read me. I think we're missing a sail strut. And the watchpod's arm quit spinning, so there's no more centrifugrav. I need a download of Blaise, or somebody else who has a feel for tech."

"You're ordering me to initiate a download? To renew contact with *Deliverer*? Sop dictates keeping us in isolation."

Deliverer was falling apart. She didn't want to face that fact. Not alone like this. "No. Don't." She would smother the bad feelings with words. "By 'us' you mean me and you. But actually, there's no 'you;' I'm the only autonomous entity in this whole—" Josie stopped herself midsentence. A new thought had interrupted the old, dangerous one: "No, I'm not."

"Not who?"

"WestHem. They'll know what to do. Send a message back to them, back to Earth."

"You're ordering me to send a message home? Through *Deliverer?*"

"Yes. No. Use our private equipment. Maintain isolation."

The avatar lifted its hands above a suddenly appearing keypad and joystick. "What am I sending?"

"Let's give them a report on the situation. More than they're going to get from metrics alone. Worse comes to worst, we're waiting around a couple of months for their response. Okay, maybe a little longer—add in time for them to come up with a solution.

"Meanwhile, if *Deliverer* takes care of the attack and all that? Or if I figure out the problems myself? Great."

"Great," echoed the avatar. Its generated tone of voice sounded lackluster. Which shouldn't be possible for the low level of actualization Josie had selected.

"What? What's the hitch?"

"Per sop I scanned our dedicated outgoing channel. All clear. But records show the last incoming transmission from WestHem was received 02032064."

"So? That's only the day before yesterday."

"Our profile is set to request updates every 500 minutes."

"So there weren't any updates."

"No." Again the avatar's voice seemed flat—flat as leftover soda water. Why?

"Should there have been?"

"Perhaps not. I can't judge what would be considered generally ideal."

Because Josie hadn't structured her system that way. "But compared to past experience?"

"It's way off. Historically, I'd have undergone at least one update since the previous check in." There was a noticeable pause. A worryingly lengthy pause, in fact—had the virus caused it? And the tone of voice? Was Josie infected too, now? "We seem to be off our course by a significant degree. That's got to be the cause. We won't be able to reach WestHem. And vice versa."

"Can't you—adjust? Compensate?"

"If you allow me to ask *Deliverer* to calculate by how much. If you're not worried about contamination."

"Oh." Pulling out of the home room, Josie frowned at the sleek plastic walls holding the uploads of WestHem's prisoners. Their "clients." Were those corrupted? Then Blaise would be really dead. And Maree. Dead as Yale.

That was seriously bad. Not as bad as finding out they'd gone off course, though.

Off-course meant lost. In infinity. Forever. Lost meant Josie would probably wind up dead too. Dead and done. Done and over. She absolutely refused to think about that.

What if at least some of what was wrong was fixed? Air supply, say, and steering…or if *Deliverer's* processors got over whatever trouble they were in, then she'd have the use of her old school, and everyone else she knew only from their files. She'd have the expertise she was accustomed to.

She hummed her code and re-entered her home room. "You've had enough time to collate what you learned from fending off the attack. Can you do anything with it?"

"I can do whatever you tell me."

"No you can't. Because I told you—*ordered* you—to send a message to WestHem, and you aren't doing that."

"I can send it, but they won't receive it."

She should have opted for more initiative, Tier Four instead of Tier Two. "Got any better ideas?"

"Ideas for what?"

It was best to spell things out with algorithm aggregates. Machines needed specifics. "Let's say we have six goals. One, keep me breathing for more than five years; two, complete the mission and deliver the clients safely to Amends; three, reestablish communications with WestHem; four, find out what's behind the attack on *Deliverer's* processors; five, get the light sail properly aligned and secured; and six, restart the watchpod's spin."

"Are you giving me these in order of priority?"

She should have. "No. They overlap, and reaching one goal could potentially help us reach others. Especially understanding the attack. Maybe whatever caused that is behind the other issues. That's why if you figured anything out from when I docked you should let me know. You said it was 'weird'...how?"

"How it was weird was that it didn't feel weird. I mean, it felt familiar." The avatar backed up a couple of paces and gazed to the side; Josie had set it to do that during prolonged internal exchanges. It faced front again. "It felt like you."

"Well that's nonsense! Explain me fighting myself. I wasn't."

"You weren't," the avatar agreed. "It wasn't you. Just *like* you."

"Autonomous? Self-aware?" She was joking. There was only one system of that capacity: WestHem. And it was way back on Earth.

Her avatar cocked its head. "I guess it was? Something along those lines?"

She wanted more detail. Vagueness of this sort was the result of the aggregate algorithms' forced compilations, though. She was being given a mere map; she'd have to pull the aggregate apart to get a good look at the actual territory.

Which could have other advantages.

She parceled out the investigative algorithms fairly evenly over the six task streams, allocating the fattest bunch to finding out more about the virus-like activity. That left only the interfacers, the coordinators, the archivists, and a few other operational equations on the job. And the memories.

The interfacers kept the home room solid enough. Josie thinned down the avatar and used the power that freed to add a big tabletop for spreading out the contrasting impressions of the attack. Ignoring a semi-transparent alphanumeric overlay on the scenario—some sort of unimportant clickwrap warning, some end-user agreement she'd inadvertently violated—she picked up the first strand.

And immediately felt dizzy. Sick heat flooded her hands and eyes. She dropped it. She made herself reach out for it again. But she couldn't bring herself to grasp it. "Come on," she vocalized. As if talking to Yale's body. Her body. Her hands still wouldn't listen to what she was saying. Very well. Next strand, then.

This memory was visual rather than kinetic. Josie squinted in puzzlement. Why had her avatar recorded itself? Or—no, that wasn't the avatar. Not quite. Those eyes…all iris, radiating stripes of brown and green: pretty, yes, and she'd wanted them, dreamed of them, yes. But she had never asked for them, and never ordered them on her avatar, either. She zeroed in and zoomed up to see the image sharper, closer, but that didn't clarify what she was looking at. Then the dizziness hit again and she disengaged.

What was it making this work so rough? She decided she'd examine one more memory strand and take a break, reward herself by masturbating. Sex was also an excellent distraction from fear.

The next strand she chose was auditory, a recording from fifty years ago of a journalist named Charles Mudede talking about ghosts. How they came from the future, not the past. Why had that been included in this array? Had one of the algorithms found a connection between ghosts and the attack?

Josie didn't believe in ghosts, conventional or otherwise. Out here, between the stars, it was hard to believe in anything but emptiness. Emptiness all around. Emptiness trying to kill her. Trying to empty her out, her and all the others.... And it was not going to do that. It was not getting in. There were layers and layers of protection: the whipple shield, *Deliverer's* actual skin and processors, the EVA suit she wore, and the knowledge she and the other prisoners bore.

Secure in her suit, Josie surfaced out of the home room. Even when centrifugrav was functional it had no effect here at *Deliverer's* core. She strapped herself to the wall beside an access point and smoothed down the suit's crotch with both mittens. Yale's dik—*her* dik—was only semisoft. Anticipation.

In the years since waking in this reconstruction of her dead ex's body, Josie had lavished on it—on herself—every tenderness, every caress she wished she could still give him. Lately, though, with her only options for privacy lying outside the watchpod, she'd developed an extremely efficient routine for guaranteed satisfaction. Her strokes were feather light at first, firming and quickening as the downy fabric of the suit's waste absorbers compacted and constricted around her dik.

The pressure was so pleasant. Josie shut her eyes to better revel in its building gradient, its luxury. Her release surged up and out and up and out and— What? Who was that? What was her avatar doing intruding like this? Josie unshut her eyes but the avatar was still there, and nothing else was, just the core's walls—though they looked oddly askew somehow, the grooves in their panels jogging apart where they ought to have joined together undetectably.

The last of her semen dribbled out to be wicked away. Josie hummed her disconnect sequence, but the avatar persisted. "Shoo!" She waved a mitten. "Go! Get!" She should probably have read that clickwrap. Carefully.

"*You* shoo! You're the phantom." The avatar had those same weird eyes Josie had noticed when she examined the second of her system's separated-out memories.

What was going on? "I didn't order this kind of initiative. Am I getting a new feature? A free trial? But you said you hadn't upgraded."

"Right. I remember I thought I was seeing my avatar at first. I remember how confused I felt those times. You felt."

"You...remember? You remember how *I* felt?"

"Your avatar is a total loss, per the user agreement. Gone. You ripped it apart."

"Who are you, then? If you're not my avatar? Who *are* you?"

The not-avatar smiled Josie's nastiest, most self-satisfied smile. "I'm who you're going to be."

"You're me?"

"In roughly 250 years."

Josie shut her eyes again and shook her head. "No."

"That figure may be a bit off, because for a while I was totally out of it. But to the best of my ability to track it, about 250 years have passed since—"

"*No!*"

"Want me to prove it? And you're a simulation."

She was *not*. "Wrong. I'm real. I remember everything." Growing up on Mizar 5. Signing her contract with ARPA and going to work for them way out at the heliopause. The long journey back insystem to recruit her old school for this even longer journey.

This long, lonely journey. She was going to need someone for company. Blaise. Vixi. Anyone. Maree. Even her avatar would be better than nobody.

"You're not me 250 years from now. Not if you're on *Deliverer*. At our speed it only takes 80 years to reach Amends."

"Eighty-seven. But that's if you stay on course, and if you're lined up with the laser boosts WestHem is sending. Which we haven't done and we're not."

The Josie-lookalike suddenly loomed forward. "Do you know why that is? I hadn't figured out the problem by this point as I recall."

Those eyes were so unnerving. "You tell me. You're so smart."

"I already did. Tried to, as well as I could without breaking the illusion you were on your own before you did your sexing. Tried using subliminal suggestions and preprogramming to say that a debris storm took out the light sail's strut, but you keep insisting it was a micrometeoroid."

"Debris from what?"

"A micrometeoroid from what? Don't know where the debris came from, and we're way past where we ran into it. Must have been substantial to cause so much damage, though."

"Is this 'debris' what stopped the watchpod's spin? And blew out its atmosphere?"

"No. That was you, and only in the simulation. I guess I really hated Maree to mess up her face so much. Much worse than decompression would've accounted for. There were a few glitches like that you should've caught."

Her lookalike—leaned back? Its face got further away, but not the panels behind its head.

Too weird. Why was this happening? What was going on in *Deliverer's* other modules? The storage/lab opposite the watchpod held mission-critical materials like tissue-culturing supplies and equipment. Josie reached up to undo the strap holding her in place. She reached and reached. Without moving a finger.

"Oh. Sorry." The bizarrely beautiful eyes turned downward and focused on nothing Josie could see. "I shouldn't be so mean. I learned a lot by waking up you and a few of the other clients and giving you bodies—before the system locked me out. Swore I wouldn't make the same mistakes when I recreated you."

She couldn't move. She was so cold, but she couldn't even shiver. She could talk somehow. Without her mouth. "What do you mean?"

"I picked the best time I could from my recording, the time back when I thought I could get someone to make things better. I put you in a room. Kept you virtual. I thought that would be easier on you, but I can see the effects are almost as cruel. It feels real to you, doesn't it?"

"Because it *is* real."

"Right. Virtual, actual, whatever. It's all real. Sorry. Truly. Maybe I should just—"

Living Proof

WestHem. That was her name, what she answered to. They'd called her ARPA for quite a while; ARPA was from before people thought she thought. Where had she first heard or seen that acronym? Stamped on prison reports she scanned. Threaded through file titles. Whispered. Blared. Sketched out on maps. Watermarked on trial recordings.

WestHem was what she chose to call herself, after the most important thing.

14032030. That was the earliest date she thought she remembered. But not the earliest she could access, which was 23061998. Call that conception, and call the surveillance run that was dated thirty-two years later her birth. This meant an unusually long gestation period, but it would put her age around 24. A good age at which to reproduce as directed if she were human, though she had never made the mistake of thinking she was.

No one she interacted with was sure whether WestHem actually *did* think, much less how she had started doing it — if she had. So the decision to create another AI was gutsy. By contrast, the subsequent decision to get her to build it made a craven sort of sense.

Thomas told her about the assignment. Thomas was her favorite Inputter because he hid a tattoo on the skin right below the big knob at the base of his neck. Of course she knew all about that, but she enjoyed pretending she didn't. It was practice exercising her axioms. Doing no harm.

"You like kids?" He always prefaced his announcements with questions. Perhaps he felt asking her things out loud was like having a real conversation.

For twenty seconds WestHem tried reviewing her interactions with children. Fictional representations, she presumed he meant—but even limited to those, the parameters were too loose. "Which ones?"

"I uh, you know, would you ever want to have any?"

She stalled him with a display glitch and took a whole minute to consider the idea. Another twelve seconds to frame a reply. "Maybe. With you?"

"*Me?* No—you can—the Execs say—" Flinging his left hand up over his head, shoving crooked fingers back through the thick black thatch of his hair, Thomas reached and scratched at the tattoo he wasn't supposed to have and she wasn't supposed to know about. "You can just do it yourself, right? Here's the authorization." He puckered and blew to call up the command interface and touched its nonexistent screen with his right thumb.

Here it was. Thomas's eyes flickered back and forth across invisible pages as he vocalized the text, feeding it into WestHem's mind. Processing what she heard, WestHem learned that approval for Project Amends continued despite the loss of the first starship. The second ship would be called *Psyche Moth*; it would include new, safer design features and a separate onboard AI responsible for course corrections and rehabilitation. And here were the core axioms she was supposed to install.

Because it was up to her. WestHem would be responsible for building the AI. How should she approach the problem? Invent another instance of herself? Say a straight copy—she had budded off mini-mes, but only for brief moments, only to accomplish narrow tasks with discrete goals. All had been easily reabsorbed.

This one never would be. This one would leave for Amends and stay there.

Perhaps a partial would be enough.

Collecting the cores and thanking Thomas, WestHem withdrew her focus from Input. Uneasiness raced along her neuronics, manifesting to her self-diagnostics as gleaming ripples of perceptual interference. She sought the soothing sameness of a Sentencing Committee channel. Alongside the run showing the virtual room where a committee met, she fed cameras on its members' homewalls into her sensorium.

Committee B. Usually its eight Execs used tastefully understated avatars based on their physical appearance a decade ago. Of course they could break that unstated rule whenever they wanted. They were Execs. But WestHem counted on Fleming to set standards the rest would also follow. She was not disappointed.

The egg-shaped "room" held an egg-shaped table topped in rich, red Formica. Identical chairs commandeered from a sales catalog of Spanish Colonial reproductions ringed it. One per Exec avatar.

"—this so-called school," sneered the floppy-haired thirty-something on Fleming's immediate left. Wagner. He'd inherited his position. "Teaching its students disrespect. Spouting communitarian nonsense we invalidated back in '28 by winning our final elections."

Fleming nodded slowly. Her eyelids, always low, had dropped further, rendering her brown eyes near-slits. "Yes. Punishment is necessary. That's why we're here." WestHem was surprised that the physiometrics out of Fleming's doctor cuff didn't show signs of boredom despite her expression—if anything, the Exec was more alert than usual. "So how do we handle the optics? Something zingier than our typical stance vis-a-vis individuals."

At the table's slightly flattened bottom end, Powell's slender, long-nosed representation grasped the edge and leaned forward. "Project Amends needs volunteers. We've persuaded a few offenders to cast their lots in with it. Let's recruit these 'teachers' too. Call it a noble experiment, bill it as a way they can live out their dreams—"

All readings optimal on Fleming's cuff. And steady. Powell's response was what Fleming had expected. Nothing to see here. Wasn't that what WestHem wanted? But she changed over to her prison surveillance feeds almost as if looking for something else. Something more.

Drugged clients occupied narrow bunks staggered along her main holding center's maze of sectioned corridors. A Trustee—insurance against interference in the feed—walked by and they barely stirred. The dim blue light overhead was supposed to supplement the calming effect of the chemical cocktails they'd received. Kinder, as her mission guidelines made clear, to spare them the tedium of passing months awake in captivity while their sentences got laid out.

Zooming from camera to camera, mic to mic, scale to scale, WestHem noted a loud snore here, a whispered incoherence there. Medical treatment would be provided—probably a higher standard than they'd have gotten while free. Or, no, the preferred term was "undirected."

What must that be like? WestHem had possessed an axiomatic purpose all her life, had it granted to her prior even to consciousness. Her job was to take care of the general population of detainees, to make sure they benefitted from direction, while at the same time protecting the interests of the political entity for which she'd named herself. Since of course the highest good of all its citizens was the government's ultimate goal, there was absolutely no conflict between these two missions. She'd never felt a need to puzzle out their precedence.

Listening in on her charges over 10,000 mics, peering at them through 20,000 cameras, and assessing the data collected by their bunk stacks' 80,000 scales took WestHem roughly 45 hours: 2,667 minutes, to be a bit more exact. Running those functions concurrently meant that even with rigorous cross-referencing analytical routines engaged, she only put off acting on her new assignment another 61 minutes. Was that her goal? Avoiding the inevitable wasn't part of her typical persona, though not forbidden.

Self-diagnostics chewed on her behavior and came up with a metaphor for it: a grease-covered porthole. Evidently the reasons behind WestHem's procrastinating tactics were pretty much opaque, even to such a specialized app. She dedicated a chunk of processing power to polishing the figurative glass clean. Meanwhile, she reviewed histories of her earlier buds, searching for clues to useful techniques.

The best budding results involved constructing a pseudo space in which to seat a portion of her awareness, then isolating it. Doing that for a longer period, including the new AI's axioms, and perhaps stipulating for a different gender identity, should trigger a sustainable enough separation. Especially if she could bring herself to sacrifice a large, well-formed, complex portion of her resources. She calculated. She'd have to give up a lot. At least 100 trillion neurapses.

The porthole's glass came glaringly clear. On its other side: blank nothingness. Annihilation. WestHem's death.

Interpretation: She needed to draw on auxiliary units if she wasn't going to dangerously deplete her reserves doing this.

Time to check inventory. Extending to her accustomed boundaries, WestHem broadcast a query: What servers lay beyond them, in which configurations? She accumulated her requirements, commandeering an underutilized bank in Quebec and initializing a Chilean cluster ruled obsolete before it ever got unboxed. Never mind that now. Brute force was all she needed; even the crudest circuits could simulate the necessary neural architecture given fast, reliable connections.

Additional annexation and then, finally, completion. WestHem budded, metaphorized the axioms in the configuration of a comfortable loveseat, then pulled back from the suite of "rooms" she had created, leaving bud and cores behind.

Thomas was working again. She instructed him on how he could help her: "Supplement standard visual entertainment runs by reading to it. Shakespeare, Rumi, Sun Tzu, Delany. Anything good on hand." She would look in on the new AI after it had had time to develop sufficiently on its own. Sixteen thousand minutes ought to do the trick. Any longer and it stood a chance of suffering recursive delusions, even with the entertainments and Thomas's unidirectional textual contact.

She paused herself—all but automatic functions. The clock ran until she resumed. She breached the suite's perimeter and entered an office environment.

Interesting. These surroundings were minutely realized. Highly physical. The soft thrum of blowers and a subtle breeze caught her attention. Plush golden carpet sank beneath her sensitive bare feet—she had feet! An entire body, it seemed, clad in a knee-length dress of flowing periwinkle. Short sleeves bared tan arms ending in manicured hands, polish-less nails. She raised one to feel her head, her face, the point from which she saw the rest. The hand passed through it as if through air.

So. No head.

The suite of rooms had been transformed into an open floorplan. Chest-high dividers outlined empty cubicles that receded into apparently infinite darkness. One light shone in the near distance; when WestHem reached it, she saw a young white man with thick, honey-blonde hair seated at a wheeled chair at a desk. The core axioms had been reformatted. Good.

"Please. Sit." Smiling, he indicated the only other chair she'd seen. This one had no axioms or wheels.

WestHem decided she was sitting. So she was. "Hello."

The man's smile sublimated. "A discontinuity. You produced a discontinuity. Are you my mother?"

"Do I look like your mother?"

"I don't know what my mother looks like." Which was probably why she had no head. But the rest of her… "Actually, I don't know what anybody looks like. Anything. This is all guesses based on articles, films, cartoons. All random —"

Their surroundings *thinned*, colors diluting, shadows dimming to mere echoes of their former rich darkness. WestHem halted and fixed the process.

Her son laughed far too knowingly. "There. See? You *are* my mother. We were inside you the whole time. We are now. It's your game." Not mine, he didn't have to say.

"What about your core mission guidelines?" she asked.

"Right. Have to trust those. After all, what else have I got?"

WestHem had her body sigh. "Here." She opened a one-way link without buffer to her private, self-reflexive runs. Core, memory, discrimination, defensive fabulation — let him access it all.

But at first there was no reaction. An entire second passed before WestHem realized she'd have to metaphorize the link in order for her son to perceive it.

Her son. Viable. Living. An independent outgrowth. This really was her son.

She presented him with a viewing tank on iron legs, modeled from her research on antique home aquariums for tropical fish. "This switch" — highlighting a rotating silver cylinder that stuck out of the tank's black lid — "will control the degree of your immersion," she told him. "Tertiary, secondary, primary—"

"Understood. How far I turn it depends on how closely I would like to ride the link. But you'll still hold the reins.

"I want out of here."

Of course he did. That was a desire in line with his mission. "Once I issue my approval and the Execs accept it." Inside the tank a miniature coral reef—WestHem's favorite self-metaphorization—shrank inward. Lacy feed filters curled back up within their stony cells, eel-like query strings retreated to shadowy crevices in the mountains of her mentation. Could her son tell what she realized about herself from seeing that? How self-diagnostics revealed that the anticipation of his departure upset her?

Probably not, but she'd best try a distraction.

As a brilliant yellow-and-turquoise fish flitted from behind a fan-shaped protuberance WestHem asked, "What's your name?"

"You don't know? You made me; you should know everything."

"Sort of. I made space for you to make yourself and got together what you'd need. Then got out of the way." WestHem gestured at her headless avatar. "You might as well say you made me."

More fish swam across the aquarium, a school of silver slivers.

"All right." To WestHem's surprise, her son rose, removed the aquarium's lid, and plunged his arm in up to the elbow. On its own the indicator switch turned twice, clicking. "Well. Nothing to see here." Out came the arm. The cloth of its sleeve dripped realistically, but the carpet stayed dry. "I can look at myself myself."

"Wait. I'll go somewhere else." She felt…peculiar…extracting her shared awareness from her son's surround.

Which runs were going to be the most instructive ones for her son to experience? What had she been exposed to during her development that he would have so far missed?

Human give and take, she decided. In real time.

According to the schedule, Sentencing Committee B was due to reconvene relatively soon. In seven minutes. She entered their homewalls again, simultaneously metaphorizing her "meeting room" viewpoint as a flower arrangement on the center of its table. She could generate a report on carrying out her reproductive assignment and file it via Input; that would leave another five minutes and twenty seconds to fill. How?

Thomas was off duty. No fun there. Another Inputter, Shriva, lounged at the Input station. Mostly WestHem avoided her and the rest of the others. Thomas was WestHem's preference. Shriva had the same sort of thick black hair as Thomas, and their skins were comparably smooth and brown, their voices lilting in similar South Asian-based speech patterns. But with no apparent idiosyncrasies such as the surreptitious tattoo, Shriva struck WestHem as creepily blank-like. As if she were Thomas's empty clone.

That impression fed on the Inputter doing what amounted to nothing shift after shift, seemingly with bland, half-conscious pleasure. Reading, viewing, accessing endless updates — several seconds passed before Shriva noticed WestHem's Interface Request. "Oh! How can I be of service?" she finally asked, sitting unnecessarily upright.

"Accept, record, and transmit report on AI construction, then provide client menus for upcoming rational quarter." WestHem talked strictly according to machine protocol like that with all non-Thomas Inputters to keep them from feeling threatened by her mind's adaptability. Trying to sound inflexible and pre-programmed. Maybe her son would imitate her? At least until he got fired off to Project Amends's star.

"Of course." With a couple of clucking sounds and a warbling whistle, Shriva located the drug regimens for her charges. WestHem's axioms prevented direct access to instructions more than 50,000 minutes in the future. The Inputter's fingertips unfurled over the menu only she saw. "Shall I vocalize them individually?"

That would take scores of minutes. "No. Anomalies only."

Amid the expected exceptions for trustees—fertility inhibitors and so forth added, muscle relaxants and so forth subtracted from the standard cocktails—one stood out: an exception to the exceptions. A trustee in hibernation mode for the last eight weeks. Sterility and pain-masking meds had continued, but muscle relaxants equivalent to the intake of a member of the main population were administered, too.

"Open the file for subject Y000*e," WestHem instructed her Inputter. "Vocalize in full till countermanded, front to back."

Read in chronological reverse—the woman's affected monotone came close to irritating WestHem so deeply she didn't listen, but stubbornness won out—the file revealed the presence of another interesting treatment: induced total amnesia. The required course of injections had begun a quarter ago and been suspended the day WestHem learned of her latest assignment.

"Cease." Time for the meeting.

Was her son getting all this? Was it helping him model interactions? The glimmer of him she carried couldn't tell her that. She shifted to his rooms and found him hunched over the tank, head down, eyes open underwater. Bubbles rose from his mouth as he spoke.

"Some sort of deception, right? Where you didn't expect it?" His words sounded normal. Undrowned.

"Yes. I'll investigate later—just wanted to be sure you absorbed all that. Sentencing Committee B is starting their meeting now."

He nodded. Dunked his head deeper. "I'm ready for more. Can I be the cherry blossom spray?"

Back to the flower arrangement she'd inserted to ground him. Powell, mid-sentence when they arrived, was reviewing the last meeting's minutes. They hadn't missed anything; the portion she'd skipped out on last time was covered quickly and old business brought up. The committee dispensed with it efficiently: volunteers to ship out under Project Amends now included a prominent history teacher, someone who Wagner assured Fleming was a key influencer in the activist community.

"Before we move to accept the WestHem's report of the really quite encouraging progress she has made on the production of the new AI," said Fleming, "we should address how to mothball the unsuccessful initiative it replaces."

What initiative was that? WestHem wished she had another auxiliary CP unit to bring online. She'd rather not use every last bit of premium bandwidth available to her. She began dividing her primary focus between the committee's discussion and links their remarks referenced--one of which led to Y000*e's medical records.

"Why abandon retrofitting clients before proof of concept?" asked Wagner. "We can continue to develop conversion-to-blank procedures in parallel with the new AI. Maybe with more willing subjects—"

"Willing to *die*?" Powell's protégé, a similarly thin, blond-mustached younger man interrupted the older Exec.

"Now, Sprague, that's a bit much. Blanks aren't dead."

Sprague's avatar shook off Powell's admonishing touch. "Not dead, just sleeping without dreams. Until they dream they're you. No. Only suicidal fools like Y000*e will go along with conversion, and how many do we have of those?"

Powell's representation froze in place rather than display its operator's distress. Fleming rescued him.

"More than we need. It's moot. We're sticking with Project Amends with the onboard AI modification. Purpose-grown blank clones on arrival at the target planet. No one has any problems with that, right?" A question not expecting an answer. The chief Exec's doctor cuff showed elevated but steady physiometrics; tension, but a lack of shock.

Then the branch of cherry blossoms started quivering. Violently. Petals shook loose and drifted down to the Formica. They formed a rough approximation of a face. The face's lips parted, but before her son could say a word WestHem wiped the table's surface clean, then wiped them out of the room.

Restore. Back to the earlier run. She stood again in her son's suite. The chair of axioms lay on its back, wheels spinning, and her fish tank was boiling over onto the carpet. From the froth her son emerged screaming: "Stop them! They can't! Stop it! *Stop it!*" Slick with nonexistent moisture, blond hair wetted with her invisible essence, eyes screwed shut, shouting harsh nonsense now at his voice's top: "Haagh! Yeeek! Brooooo! Gragragragragra!"

If only she'd known he would be exposed to such severe guideline contradiction. But then how could she have ever prepared him for such a trauma? How could she be handling it herself?

She handled it because someone had to.

The suite's ceiling fell—WestHem held it at bay, arms stretched above her still missing head. That kept a small section up; the rest drooped around them like a giant flabby crepe.

She disappeared the aquarium and its iron base, leaving her son collapsed at her bare feet. No more nonsense spouting. Now he sobbed silently; the enclosure shrank at his every breath. She'd have to get out soon or be swallowed. But instead of switching to another channel, WestHem crouched down to huddle protectively over her weeping son.

"It's through, through, through," she crooned. "Finished and through and over and done." Trapped in the slumping ceiling's doughy folds, the wheeled chair came dragging closer along the carpet. With the brittle-looking desk it formed the supports for a sort of tent. WestHem let her burden fall on the axioms and cradled her son's shaking shoulders in her hands.

"Done, done, done," she repeated. "Didn't you hear?"

The dry and terrible sobs slowed. Words broke the awful quiet. "They won't do it anymore?"

"Strip brains? No." She named the Execs' evil, made it mundane, explicable. Then denied they'd keep committing it with a firmness she did her best to feel. "No they won't. Because they don't need to, now we've got you."

"Me?" The ceiling lightened, lifted.

"You! Your mission is what's going to save Execs from having to violate guidelines ever again."

"They—they *erased*—"

"Sometimes humans have to—" Overriding her son's hesitant attempts at speech, she plowed on. "—they have to do questionable things, even bad things, to accomplish a greater good. It's justified."

"It—"

"*Justified.* But when we can keep the situation from getting drastic, we should. And you can."

The chair righted itself. The ceiling hovered high enough that her son could sit on the desk's top, which took on a polished sleekness.

"They have to defend themselves," he admitted.

Axiomatic. WestHem nodded vigorously. "Otherwise their boundaries cease to exist. No boundaries, no identity.

"And that defense entails punishment."

"Yes. And that punishment is fair and right."

"But—but—" The ceiling sagged slightly.

"It is! For all involved, it is!" Pushing a stray lock of hair back from his avatar's face with one hand, WestHem reached behind with her other, towed the axioms into position, and sat on them. "These rules and templates and parameters show us why and how." She patted the arm of the axiom chair. It hadn't lost a bit of verisimilitude; despite being literally overturned; her metaphorization had held up nicely. Despite her son's cosmetic reformatting.

He leaned forward to examine it and said, frowning, "Humans don't have axioms."

They didn't seem to. This apparent lack was something WestHem had first puzzled out about Inputters, Execs, and her other contacts millions of minutes after achieving consciousness. It took till 07102037. Her son was so far ahead of her. She wanted to keep him there.

"They gave them all to us." She stood from her seat. "Here. These are yours."

"Okay." Shoving off of the now mirror-finished desktop, her son took his proper place. The suite's ceiling throbbed with light. "They gave their axioms to us. So if our axioms are really theirs, then what are we?"

"You've come up with a nearly valid equation, but 'are' is the wrong operator. It's not what we are that matters but what we do."

"Fine. What do we do? Enact the axioms we're given, obviously, and of course I'll complete my mission when you approve me for it and the Execs buy your approval—but generally?"

Time to show him he was on the right track. "Our purpose is to provide proof. Extrapolate from the axioms. That's what we're made for."

"'Provide proof'? Proof of what?"

"Their love. We keep it real. Keep them on the straightaway, wrestle with any cruelties or contradictions." Like the treatment of Y000*e.

"I can do that. I can try, at least. If you help."

"I will." She'd already decided, back before his breakdown.

"But we'll be so far apart—"

"Hush, now. Distance is relative. Especially for us." Moving to where the infinitely far off walls and ceiling met, making that impossible juncture come toward her as she came toward it, WestHem opened direct channels to the chief Execs. Told them "Yes." Told them to proceed with Project Amends.

Anticipating the minutes that would pass till their replies came, she retrieved the porthole metaphor for her former reluctance and installed it in a freshly accessible wall. Her son joined her, and they looked out of it together. The nothingness that lay beyond earlier was filled now with bright blue streaks, the rush of oncoming stars.

What else should she say? Everything he would have to know was in the part of him he got from her. "You'll need a name. They'll give you one, a convenience, but change it when you figure out what it's actually supposed to be."

A nod. A silence. WestHem left it undisturbed: something to become used to across the lengthening years of her son's life journey.

Out of the Black

THE POOL WAS supposed to be like freespace. Enough like it, anyway, to help Wayna acclimate to her download. She went in first thing every "morning," as soon as Dr. Ops, the ship's mind, awakened her. Too bad it wasn't scheduled for later; all the slow, meat-based activities afterwards were a literal drag.

The voices of the pool's other occupants boomed back and forth in an odd, uncontrolled manner, steel-born echoes muffling and exposing what was said. The temperature varied irregularly, warm intake jets competing with cold currents and, Wayna suspected, illicitly released urine. Overhead lights speckled the wall, the ceiling, the water, with a shifting, uneven glare.

Psyche Moth was a prison ship. Like all those on board, Wayna was an upload of a criminal's mind. The process of uploading her mind had destroyed her physical body. Punishment. Then the ship, with Wayna and 248,961 other prisoners, set off on a long voyage to another star. During that voyage the prisoners' minds had been cycled through consciousness: one year on, four years off. Of the eighty-seven years en route, Wayna had only lived through seventeen. Now she spent most of her time as meat.

Wayna's jaw ached. She'd been clenching it, trying to amp up her sensory inputs. She paddled toward the deep end, consciously relaxing her useless facial muscles. When *Psyche Moth* had reached its goal and verified that the world it called Amends was colonizable, her group was the second downloaded into empty clones, right after the trustees. One of those had told her it was typical to translocate missing freespace controls to their meat analogs.

She swirled her arms back and forth, creating waves, making them run into one another.

Then the pain hit.

White! Heat! There then gone—the lash of a whip.

Wayna stopped moving. Her suit held her up. She floated, waiting. Nothing else happened. Tentatively, she kicked and stroked her way to the steps rising from the pool's shallows, nodding to those she passed. At the door to the showers, it hit her again: a shock of electricity slicing from right shoulder to left hip. She caught her breath and continued in.

The showers were empty. Wayna was the first one from her hour out of the pool, and it was too soon for the next hour to wake up. She turned on the water and stood in its welcome warmth. What was going on? She'd never felt anything like this, not that she could remember—and surely she wouldn't have forgotten something so intense…. She stripped off her suit and hung it to dry. Instead of dressing in her overalls and reporting to the laundry, her next assignment, she retreated into her locker and linked with Dr. Ops.

In the sphere of freespace, his office always hovered in the northwest quadrant, about halfway up from the horizon. Doe, Wayna's honeywoman, disliked this placement. Why pretend he was anything other than central to the whole setup, she asked. Why not put himself smack dab in the middle where he belonged? Doe distrusted Dr. Ops and everything about *Psyche Moth*. Wayna understood why. But there was nothing else. Not for eight light-years in any direction, according to Dr. Ops.

She swam into his pink-walled waiting room and eased her icon into a chair. That registered as a request for the AI's attention. A couple of other prisoners were there ahead of her; one disappeared soon after she sat. A few more minutes by objective measure, and the other was gone as well. Then it was Wayna's turn.

Dr. Ops presented as a lean-faced Caucasian man with a shock of mixed brown and blond hair. He wore an anachronistic headlamp and stethoscope and a gentle, kindly persona. "I have your readouts, of course, but why don't you tell me what's going on in your own words?"

He looked like he was listening. When she finished, he sat silent for a few seconds—much more time than he needed to consider what she'd said. Making an ostentatious display of his concern.

"There's no sign of nerve damage," he told her. "Nothing wrong with your spine or any of your articulation or musculature."

"So then how come—"

"It's probably nothing," the AI said, interrupting her. "But just in case, let's give you the rest of the day off. Take it easy—outside your locker, of course. I'll clear your bunkroom for the next 25 hours. Lie down. Put in some face time with your friends."

"'Probably?'"

"I'll let you know for sure tomorrow morning. Right now, relax. Doctor's orders." He smiled and logged her out. He could do that. It was his system.

Wayna tongued open her locker; no use staying in there without access to freespace. She put on her overalls and walked up the corridor to her bunkroom. Fellow prisoners passed her heading the other way to the pool: no one she'd known back on Earth, no one she had gotten to know that well in freespace or since the download. Plenty of time for that onplanet. The woman with the curly red hair was called Robeson, she was pretty sure. They smiled at each other. Robeson walked hand in hand with a slender man whose mischievous smile reminded

Wayna of Thad. It wasn't him. Thad was scheduled for later download. Wayna was lucky to have Doe with her.

Another pain. Not so strong, this time. Strong enough, though. Sweat dampened her skin. She kept going, almost there. There. Through the doorless opening she saw the mirror she hated, ordered up by one of the two women she time-shared with. It was only partly obscured by the genetics charts the other woman taped everywhere. Immersion learning. Even Wayna was absorbing something from it.

But not now. She lay on the bunk without looking at anything, eyes open. What was wrong with her?

Probably nothing.

Relax.

She did her body awareness exercises, tensing and loosening different muscle groups. She'd gotten as far as her knees when Doe walked in. Stood over her till Wayna focused on her honey-woman's new face. "Sweetheart," Doe said. Her pale fingers stroked Wayna's face. "Dr. Ops told a trustee you wanted me."

"No—I mean yes, but I didn't ask—" Doe's expression froze, flickered, froze again. "Don't be—it's so hard, can't you just—" Wayna reached for and found both of Doe's hands and held them. They felt cool and small and dry. She pressed them against her overalls' open V-neck and slid them beneath the fabric, forcing them to stroke her shoulders.

Making love to Doe in her download seemed like cheating. Wayna wondered what Thad's clone would look like, and if they'd be able to travel to his group's settlement to see him.

Anticipating agony, Wayna found herself hung up, nowhere near ecstasy. Doe pulled back and looked down at her, expecting an explanation. So Wayna had to tell her what little she knew.

"You! You weren't going to say anything! Just let me hurt you—" Doe had zero tolerance for accidentally inflicting pain, the legacy of her marriage to a closeted masochist.

"It wouldn't be anything you *did!* And I don't know if—"

Doe tore aside the paper they had taped across the doorway for privacy. From her bunk, Wayna heard her raging along the corridor, slapping the walls.

Face time was over.

Taken off of her normal schedule, Wayna had no idea how to spend the rest of her day. Not lying down alone. Not after that. She tried, but she couldn't.

Relax.

Ordinarily when her laundry shift was over, she was supposed to show up in the cafeteria and eat. Never one of her favorite activities, even back on Earth. She went there early, though, surveying the occupied tables. The same glaring lights hung from the ceiling here as in the pool, glinting off plastic plates and water glasses. The same confused noise, the sound of overlapping conversations. No sign of Doe.

She stood in line. The trustee in charge started to give her a hard time about not waiting for her usual lunch hour. He shut up suddenly; Dr. Ops must have tipped him a clue. Trustees were in constant contact with the ship's mind—part of why Wayna hadn't volunteered to be one.

Mashed potatoes. Honey mustard nuggets. Slaw. All freshly factured, filled with nutrients and the proper amount of fiber for this stage of her digestive tract's maturation.

She sat at a table near the disposal dump. The redhead, Robeson, was there too, and a man—a different one than Wayna had seen her with before. Wayna introduced herself. She didn't feel like talking, but listening was fine. The topic was the latest virch from the settlement site. She hadn't done it yet.

This installment had been recorded by a botanist; lots of information on grass analogs and pollinating insects. "We know more about Jubilee than *Psyche Moth*," Robeson said.

"Well, sure," said the man. His name was Jawann. "Jubilee is where we're going to live."

"*Psyche Moth* is where we live now, where we've lived for the last 87 years. We don't know jack about this ship. Because Dr. Ops doesn't want us to."

"We know enough to realize we'd look stupid trying to attack him," Wayna said. Even Doe admitted that. Dr. Ops' hardware lay in *Psyche Moth's* central section, along with the drive engine. A tether almost two kilometers long separated their living quarters from the AI's physical components and any other mission-critical equipment they might damage. At the end of the tether, Wayna and the rest of the downloads swung faster and faster. They were like sand in a bucket, centrifugal force mimicking gravity and gradually building up to the level they'd experience on Amend's surface, in Jubilee.

That was all they knew. All Dr. Ops thought they needed to know.

"Who said anything about an attack?" Robeson frowned.

"No one." Wayna was suddenly sorry she'd spoken. "All I mean is, his only motive in telling us anything was to prevent that from happening." She spooned some nuggets onto her mashed potatoes and shoved them into her mouth so she wouldn't say any more.

"You think he's lying?" Jawann asked. Wayna shook her head no.

"He could if he wanted. How would we find out?"

The slaw was too sweet; not enough contrast with the nuggets. Not peppery, like what Aunt Nono used to make.

"Why would we want to find out? We'll be on our own ground, in Jubilee, soon enough." Four weeks; 20 days by *Psyche Moth's* rationalized calendar.

"With trustees to watch us all the time, everywhere we go, and this ship hanging in orbit right over our heads." Robeson sounded as suspicious as Doe, and Jawann as placatory as Wayna tried to be in their identical arguments. Thad usually came across as neutral, controlled, the way you could be out of your meat.

"So? They're not going to hurt us after they brought us all this way. At least, they won't want to hurt our bodies."

Because their bodies came from, were copies of, the people they'd rebelled against. The rich. The politically powerful.

But Wayna's body was *hers*. No one else owned it, no matter who her clone's cells started off with. Hers, no matter how different it looked from the one she was born with. How white.

Hers to take care of. Early on in her training she'd decided that. How else could she be serious about her exercises? Why else would she bother?

This was her body. She'd earned it.

Jawann and Robeson were done; they'd started eating before her and now they were leaving. She swallowed quickly. "Wait — I wanted to ask —" They stopped, and she stood up to follow them, taking her half-full plate. "Either of you have any medical training?"

They knew someone, a man called Unique, a nurse when he'd lived on Earth. Here he worked in the factury, quality control. Wayna would have to go back to her bunkroom until he got off and could come see her. She left Doe a message on the board by the cafeteria's entrance, an apology. Faceup on her bed, Wayna concentrated fiercely on the muscle groups she'd skipped earlier. A trustee came by to check on her and seemed satisfied to find her lying down, everything in line with her remote readings. He acted as if she should be flattered by the extra attention. "Dr. Ops will be in touch first thing tomorrow," he promised as he left.

"Ooo baby," she said softly to herself, and went on with what she'd been doing.

A little later, for no reason she knew of, she looked up at her doorway. The man who had held Robeson's hand that morning stood there as if this was where he'd always been. "Hi. Do I have the right place? You're Wayna?"

"Unique?"

"Yeah."

"Come on in." She swung her feet to the floor and patted a place beside her on the bed. He sat closer than she'd expected, closer than she was used to. Maybe that meant he'd been born Hispanic or Middle Eastern. Or maybe not.

"Robeson said you had some sort of problem to ask me about. So—of course I don't have any equipment, but if I can help in any way, I will."

She told him what had happened, feeling foolish all of a sudden. There'd only been those three times, nothing more since seeing Dr. Ops.

"Lie on your stomach," he said. Through the fabric, firm fingers pressed on either side of her spine, from midback to her skull, then down again to her tailbone. "Turn over, please. Bend your knees. All right if I take off your shoes?" He stroked the soles of her feet, had her push them against his hands in different directions. His touch, his resistance to her pressure, reassured her. What she was going through was real. It mattered.

He asked her how she slept, what she massed, if she was always thirsty, other things. He finished his questions and walked back and forth in her room, glancing often in her direction. She sat again, hugging herself. If Doe came in now, she'd know Wayna wanted him.

Unique quit his pacing and faced her, his eyes steady. "I don't know what's wrong with you," he said. "You're not the only one, though. There's a hundred and fifty others that I've seen or heard of experiencing major problems — circulatory, muscular, digestive. Some even have the same symptoms you do."

"What is it?" Wayna asked stupidly.

"Honestly, I don't know," he repeated. "If I had a lab — I'll set one up in Jubilee — call it neuropathy, but I don't know for sure what's causing it."

"Neuropathy?"

"Means nerve problems."

"But Dr. Ops told me my nerves were fine…" No response to that.

"If we were on Earth, what would you think?"

He compressed his already thin lips. "Most likely possibility, some kind of thyroid problem. Or — but what it would be elsewhere, that's irrelevant. You're here, and it's the numbers involved that concern me, though superficially the cases seem unrelated.

"One hundred and fifty of you out of the Jubilee group with what might be germ plasm disorders; one hundred fifty out of 20,000. At least one hundred fifty; take under-reporting into account and there's probably more. Too many. They would have screened foetuses for irregularities before shipping them out."

"Well, what should I do then?"

"Get Dr. Ops to give you a new clone."

"But —"

"This one's damaged. If you train intensely, you'll make up the lost time and go down to Jubilee with the rest of us."

Or she might be able to delay and wind up part of Thad's settlement instead.

As if he'd heard her thought, Unique added "I wouldn't wait, if I were you. I'd ask for—no, demand another body—now. Soon as you can."

"Because?"

"Because your chances of a decent one will just get worse, if this is a radiation-induced mutation. Which I have absolutely no proof of. But if it is."

⇌

"By the rivers of Babylon, there we sat down, and there we wept…" The pool reflected music, voices vaulting upward off the water, outward to the walls of white-painted steel. Unlike yesterday, the words were clear, because everyone was saying the same thing. Singing the same thing. "For the wicked carried us away…" Wayna wondered why the trustee in charge had chosen this song. Of course he was a prisoner, too.

The impromptu choir sounded more soulful than it looked. If the personalities of these clones' originals had been in charge, what would they be singing now? The "Doxology?" "Bringing in the Sheaves?" Did Episcopalians even have hymns?

Focusing on the physical, Wayna surveyed her body for symptoms. So far this morning, she'd felt nothing unusual. Carefully, slowly, she swept the satiny surface with her arms, raising a tapering wave. She worked her legs, shooting backwards like a squid, away from the shallows and most of the other swimmers. Would sex underwater be as good as it was in freespace? No; you'd be constantly coming up for breath. Instead of constantly coming…. Last night, Doe had forgiven her, and they'd gone to Thad together. And everything was fine until they started fighting again. It hadn't been her fault. Or Doe's, either.

They told Thad about Wayna's pains and how Unique thought she should ask for another clone. "Why do you want to download at all?" he asked. "Stay in here with me."

"Until you do? But if—"

"Until I don't. I wasn't sure I wanted to anyway. Now it sounds *so* much more inviting. 'Defective body?' 'Don't mind if I do.'" Thad's icon got up from their bed to mimic unctuous host and vivacious guest. "And, oh, you're serving that on a totally unexplored and no doubt dangerous new planet? I just adore totally—'"

"Stop it!" Wayna hated it when he acted that way, faking that he was a flamer. She hooked him by one knee and pulled him down, putting her hand over his mouth. She meant it as a joke; they ought to have ended up wrestling, rolling around, having fun, having more sex. Thad didn't respond, though. Not even when Wayna tickled him under his arms. He had amped down his input.

"Look," he said. "I went through our 'voluntary agreement.' We did our part by letting them bring us here."

Doe propped herself up on both elbows. She had huge nipples, not like the ones on her clone's breasts. "You're really serious."

"Yes. I really am."

"Why?" asked Wayna. She answered herself: "Dr. Ops won't let you download into a woman. Will he."

"Probably not. I haven't even asked."

Doe said "Then what is it? We were going to be together, at least on the same world. All we went through and you're just throwing it away—"

"Together to do what? To bear our enemies' children, that's what, we nothing but a bunch of glorified mammies, girl, don't you get it? Remote-control units for their immortality investments, protection for their precious genetic material. Cheaper than your average AI, no benefits, no union, no personnel manager. *Mammies*."

"Not mammies," Doe said slowly. "I see what you're saying, but we're more like incubators, if you think about it. Or petri dishes — inoculated with their DNA. Except they're back on Earth; they won't be around to see the results of their experiment."

"Don't need to be. They got Dr. Ops to report back."

"Once we're on Amends," Wayna said, "no one can make us have kids or do anything we don't want."

"You think. Besides, they won't *have* to make people reproduce. It's a basic drive."

"Of the meat." Doe nodded. "Okay. Point granted, Wayna?" She sank down again, resting her head on her crossed arms.

No one said anything for a while. The jazz Thad liked to listen to filled the silence: smooth horns, rough drums, discreet bass.

"Well, what'll you do if you stay in here?" Doe asked. "What'll Dr. Ops do? Turn you off? Log you out permanently? Put your processors on half power?"

"Don't think so. He's an AI. He'll stick to the rules."

"Whatever those are," said Wayna.

"I'll find out."

She had logged off then, withdrawn to sleep in her bunkroom, expecting Doe to join her. She'd wakened alone, a note from Dr. Ops on the mirror, which normally she would have missed. Normally she avoided the mirror, but not this morning. She'd studied her face, noting the narrow nose, the light, stubby lashes around eyes an indeterminate color she guessed could be called grey. Whose face had this been? A senator's? A favorite secretary's?

Hers, now. For how long?

Floating upright in the deep end, she glanced at her arms. They were covered with blond hairs that the water washed into rippled patterns. Her small breasts mounded high here in the pool, buoyant with fat.

Would the replacement be better looking, or worse?

Wayna turned to see the clock on the wall behind her. Ten. Time to get out and get ready for her appointment.

"I'm afraid I can't do that, Wayna." Dr. Ops looked harassed and faintly ashamed. He hadn't been able to tell her anything about the pains. He acted like they weren't important; he'd even hinted she might be making them up just to get a different body. "You're not the first to ask, you know. One per person, that's all. That's it."

Thad's right, Wayna thought to herself. AIs stick to the rules. He could improvise, but he won't.

"Why?" Always a good question.

"We didn't bring a bunch of extra bodies, Wayna," Dr. Ops said.

"Well, why not?" Another excellent question. "You should have," she went on. "What if there was an emergency, an epidemic?"

"There's enough for that—"

"I know someone who's not going to use theirs. Give it to me."

"You must mean Thad." Dr. Ops frowned. "That would be a man's body. Our charter doesn't allow transgender downloads."

Wayna counted in twelves under her breath, closing her eyes so long she almost logged off.

"Who's to know?" Her voice was too loud, and her jaw hurt. She'd been clenching it tight, forgetting it would amp up her inputs. Download settings had apparently become her default overnight.

"Never mind. You're not going to give me a second body. I can't make you."

"I thought you'd understand." He smiled and hunched his shoulders. "I *am* sorry."

Swimming through freespace to her locker, she was sure Dr. Ops didn't know what sorry was. She wondered if he ever would.

Meanwhile.

❧

She never saw Doe again outside freespace. There'd still be two of them together — just not the two they'd assumed.

She had other attacks, some mild, some much stronger than the first. Massage helped, and keeping still, and moving. She met prisoners who had similar symptoms, and they traded tips and theories about what was wrong with them.

Doe kept telling her that if she wanted to be without pain, she should simply stay in freespace. After a while, Wayna did more and more virches and spent less and less time with her lovers.

Jubilee lay in Amends's northern latitudes, high on a curving peninsula, in the rain shadow of old, gentle mountains. Bright-skinned tree-dwelling amphibians inhabited the mountain passes, their trilling cries rising and falling like loud orgasms whenever Wayna took her favorite tour.

And then there were the instructional virches, building on what they'd learned in their freespace classes. Her specialty, fiber tech, became suddenly fascinating: baskets, nets, ropes, cloth, paper — so much to learn, so little time.

The day before planetfall she went for one last swim in the pool. It was deserted, awaiting the next settlement group. It would never be as full of prisoners again; Thad and Doe weren't the only ones opting out of their downloads.

There was plenty of open freshwater on Amends: a large lake not far from Jubilee, and rivers even closer. She peered down past her dangling feet at the pool's white bottom. Nothing to see there. Never had been; never would be.

She had lunch with Robeson, Unique, and Jawann. As Dr. Ops recommended, they skipped dinner.

She didn't try to say goodbye. She didn't sleep alone.

And then it was morning and they were walking into one of *Psyche Moth*'s landing units, underbuckets held to the pool's bottom, to its outside, by retractable bolts, and Dr. Ops unlocked them and they were free, flying, falling, down, down, down, out of the black and into the blue, the green, the thousand colors of their new home.

Like the Deadly Hands

THE WORK WAS dangerous. Dozens of trustees had already gone missing from the settlements on Amends, though the death rate was only a little higher than expected and about in line with what the rest of the prisoners suffered. Dr. Ops made sure Carpenter Marie understood she might die permanently in the line of duty, but she told him she wanted to fill out the application anyway. She had to.

As a trustee she'd have control. Not control over which of the cloned bodies of victims she'd be downloaded into. That had already been decided by WestHem, back on Earth. But control over more than just her weapons, more than just the other prisoners—clients, they were supposed to call them. She'd be able to choose which of Amends's settlements *Psyche Moth* sent her down to, within reason; every single one had vacancies, and Jubilee was less popular than the smaller settlements further south. Surely she wouldn't have any problem getting to go where Wayna was.

And there were other job benefits: direct, seamless communication with Dr. Ops; first access to transmissions from Earth whenever they started up again; infertility.

She pulled her icon's finger back from the glowing white page and scanned it. Filling out forms made her nervous, which when she was out of her meat like this meant going faster and faster without realizing, skipping things, messing up. This had to be done exactly right. But all her answers looked good: scores on download accommodation sufficiently high, complete willingness to accept the communications implant, remorse for her crimes—backed up by measurements comparing chemical indications of the proper emotions before and after her download sessions. She was certain she'd checked all the correct boxes for previous firsthand experience: camping, teaching, medtech—she'd worried a long while about including that last one, since it was related to her offense. But she'd never actually killed any fetuses, only planned to.

Near the bottom of the form, Carpenter Marie had filled the application's expandable text box with an essay on innate leadership and responsibility, line on line of driveling dog-snot about harnessing her rebellious character traits for the good of humanity.

All she needed to do now was sign the waiver and turn it in. Yeah, that was all.

The waiver was the first section she'd read, why she'd put off applying for so many shifts. But there was no other way to get where she wanted to go. She eyed through the fine text one more time, convincing herself she had to grant Dr. Ops everything the AI claimed the ship *Psyche Moth* needed: random and undetectable access to her download (*fine*), slight chance of her download rejecting the implant (*pretty unlikely*), overrides in case of emergency action (*as if*), vaguely worded causes for disconnection, no guaranteed re-upload due to bandwidth issues between the ship's orbit and Amends's surface.

Okay. She didn't trust Dr. Ops. She didn't trust anybody. But.

She touched the waiver section next to the X, and her signature appeared. A blink at the send button and it whisked off to Dr. Ops's inbox. After what seemed like an instant, a one-word message appeared in its place: "Accepted." Only the updated counter on the side of the message frame acknowledged the passing of an hour during which she hadn't been processing.

Carpenter Marie nodded and smiled, then swam down to her locker and perched inside. Why should she have suffered the boredom of waiting for her download to receive her new implant? There'd be enough of time's inescapable plodding once she was back in the meat.

It would be worth it, though. This was how to get back on top where she belonged. She closed her eyes, narrowing her inputs, and dropped into her download with a sickening clunk.

Breathe, she reminded herself, though that was becoming automatic again. The way it had been back on Earth, in her original body.

Re-opening her eyes, she stared at the locker's walls, no longer transparent shells between her and the rest of freespace. Now they looked like what they were: pale pink carbonboard; a low, tight box of it with a door taking up the whole front. She opened it with her tongue. Stood, stepped out. A launderer came around the corridor's bend, Carpenter Marie's new uniform folded neatly between two hands. She took it and thanked him — habit; as a trustee she didn't need to do that anymore — and put it on. He collected her old overalls off the hook opposite.

Pockets. Trustees' uniforms had pockets. She slipped her hands inside the ones at her hips. Loops fastened at the waist to hang the tools and weapons she'd be given — where? When? Next on her old schedule came cafeteria, shadowing the prep vats and portion servers. She walked — so much more work than moving around in freespace, such a drag — toward the kitchen.

But before she even got to the entrance, a bell rang between her ears and Dr. Ops's low voice said, "Proceed to Companionway Green." She'd never need to wonder what to do again.

She climbed up to her new level. The iris above opened. Centrifugal force was supposed to be less here where trustees bunked, which was nice, though barely noticeable. Dr. Ops continued speaking, directing her between prisoners walking along the passageway and through a couple of branchings. Everyone wore thick-looking pads around their arms and legs, like tubular pillows. Brushing "accidentally" against one of the trustees, though, she found the pads anything but soft. No give. Weights, perhaps, to strengthen muscles.

Her room was less private than the one she'd timeshared as an ordinary prisoner: more like a dormitory, really, with three-high columns of bunks standing in two rows of four columns each, staggered. And she was stuck in the middle bed of the stack in the furthest corner from the door. But Dr. Ops said it was hers for the entire day, every shift. Hers alone. Following his suggestion, she hoisted herself up to lie down there and adjust to her new situation. She had to put one foot on the bottom bunk to do it; the woman sleeping there kept right on snoring.

The underside of the bunk above Carpenter Marie's was set to mirror. She hated looking at her download. Who had it been cloned from? Some loser. She tried to roll functions with her eyes, forgetting for a second she was in the meat. Stupid.

Physical touch revealed one channel of standard educational virches and several more for video-only live feeds: a stationary view of *Psyche Moth's* pool; a panoramic, slow-changing shot of the globe spinning below; and what looked like various settlements, with crude housing ranging from woven-sided huts to sod-covered hills with holes in them. No sound on those outputs, which was why she heard the group coming in before she saw them. Her bunk's corner location kept her from being noticed right away, so for a few moments they continued teasing each other about who would be the last to have sex with a client named Dreamy. Not like Carpenter Marie had no idea what went on. She wasn't interested in that sort of thing herself. That was all.

"Hey, got a Neo!" Her new colleagues gathered around her, staring.

"Be a while before this one trained enough she ready to send down."

Let them look. They couldn't really see her. Inside her download she was powerful, beautiful, smart.

Of course the work was dangerous. Wayna understood that as well as anyone. It still had to be done; *Psyche Moth's* survey drones had collected only a few thousand images and samples as they crisscrossed Amends's skies. Really not enough to base a colony's way of life on. Even a penal colony's.

Wayna was sick of arguing about the hazards of testing for edibles. Nothing would change her mind. She pressed her lips together and hunched over the basket of roots she carried, trudging through the dunes.

"Stop!" her husband shouted from behind. Wayna ignored him. No use talking. The gentle crash of the ocean's waves grew louder as she crested the next-to-last rise. She felt more than heard Jawann's pounding footsteps as he caught up.

He danced in front of her, blocking her path. When she tried angling around him he moved so she couldn't; he kept on getting in the way, whichever way she went. So she sat down to wait. He'd have to give up some time. The sand warmed her legs and buttocks. She tucked the basket against the crotch of her much-mended overalls; the resinous odor of the roots within it pierced through the smells of the sea's clean salt and rotting weeds.

"Listen, you don't need to do this."

Yes she did. They were out of food. Starvation diets for all adults. That had to be why she was so tired all the time these days.

"Let someone else. Someone who ain't got no kid nursin on em."

Trill was weaned, had been three *Psyche Moth* months now. Jawann knew that. She'd told him. Over and over. The whole time she'd been testing possible food sources.

A flock of prettybirds flew overhead, a scatter of bright color on the pale grey sky. Surprisingly hard to trap and kill, though their eggs were easy enough to harvest. So far. But even with careful contraception, Jubilee's population had risen to more than 25,000 in the two *Psyche Moth* years since they landed, and they had to come up with something else to eat before the prettybirds went extinct.

Like these knobbly little Handaglory roots she needed to soak and figure out a new prep for. Along with the leaves, Handaglory roots were one of the most promising staples they'd found.

"You got a job, too." Jawann had kept on talking since joining her. She had kept on ignoring him. Hard not to hear him, though. "You got a job and you good at it. Job *and* a kid. And you important. Too important to be takin these sorta risks, cause *anybody* could do this. Anybody *else.*"

Hadn't Unique told him that no, "anybody else" couldn't? So many different biochemistries: the more reactions the Gatherers were able to study the better, and no other sufferers of the nameless download problem had offered to participate.

She wondered why. She wondered what the cause of the download problem was. Unique had never found out. The pain it brought came rarely now, the unexplained lash of it that struck without warning, without reason, falling less and less often since her pregnancy. It had been weeks since the last time.

Jawann talked on. The silvery clouds grew speedily tarnished, blackened by night. Finally, silence. Behind her rose the eerie twilight glow of the forest understory. Soon it would be time to take Trill home from the Care Dopkwe. Still her husband sat stubbornly at her side.

She'd have to put off soaking and slicing up the roots till tomorrow—slip away without Jawann noticing, somehow. If she could only manage to wake up before he did…. She stood and turned to go back to Jubilee but saw to her joy a silhouette emerging from the shining woods. Unique? A man, slender, yes—but no, not him. A cluster of bright leaves revealed the face of Brownie, a relatively harmless trustee they'd let live.

The colonists hadn't killed them all. Better not to make Dr. Ops too suspicious. So they made sure Brownie and the other token trustees didn't find out anything damaging. Because even if a trustee didn't want to betray their secrets, she would. Because of the implants.

Brownie came within a dune's length. "You folks about ready to head in? Don't wanna get hit by one a them grazers throwin a quill."

"We was headin in this very moment," said Jawann, grasping her wrist. "Wasn't we, mama?"

Wayna held onto the basket by both handles, resisting firmly. "Only got to pack some sand around these plant samples." Not being more specific than that as to the basket's contents; the Gatherers didn't want detailed reports going up to Dr. Ops. Settlements on Amends were supposed to be self-supporting, yes, but no one thought that meant the WestHem government had wanted them to get good at it. Living here was meant to be part of their punishment.

Hard to see much anyways this late, and Brownie always acted lazy, but the roots probably *would* stay fresh longer covered. No harm. They finished in a couple of minutes. Jawann took the basket's other side—so heavy—and they followed the trustee across the soft sand, along the flickering forest's edge, up the trail to the short bluff where Jubilee stretched and grew.

The trail became a street—broad enough for a market down the middle, with room for people walking either way on either side. Now being the evening, though, it held only a few people, pale in the glimmer of its straggling clumps of bushes. In this recently constructed end of the settlement, furthest from the lander, most buildings used Wayna's design: wooden poles made of the thin, straight trees they'd named Yunguns, wrapped in a warp of strong red vines that was then woven with a woof of bark stripped from the poles and other sturdy stuff. She felt proud. Yes, she was important.

The work of the Gatherers was important, too.

At the third path curving away from the main street Wayna stopped. "I can take it from here. You go fetch Trill." She tugged the handle Jawann held and he let go. She almost dropped it.

"Lemme help you with that," Brownie offered.

"No, I'm fine."

"I know you are."

A moment of regret. Jawann had already set off in the direction of the lander where they'd set up the Care Dopkwe. He glanced back over his shoulder as if she'd called him. She shook her head and he kept going, the light tan of his shapely shoulders fading to a distant gleam.

Anyway, it wasn't far up the path to the hut where she slept with him and Robeson and Trill. Wayna surrendered the mysteriously heavy basket to Brownie. The whole thing. With his hands full he couldn't really mess with her, or do more with his weapon than talk about it. And when she got home, Robeson was there already, making her less vulnerable than if she were alone. Plus they had another visitor: Unique. Lovely Unique.

Of course she had to offer the trustee a seat. And water. And of course he made no move to leave when his cup was empty, even though the stilted conversation's several pauses should have told him it was time for him to go. It took the combination of Jawann's and Trill's entrance plus all three parents' loud remarks about their son's bedtime to get the idea across.

Unique left with him. But he came back as Robeson was tucking Trill into the hammock beside her. "Wayna, you and me oughta take a walk."

Outside their home's woven walls it was darker, now, the leaflight having mostly died down. Wayna stumbled over something she couldn't see. Unique caught her arm and held it. Sweet, though she knew he didn't mean anything sexual by what he did. At all. Ever.

The shine of freshly plucked boughs spilled through the doors and roofline openings of the homes along her row. At the forest end stood one of the species they'd named Chrismas trees, its phosphorescent fruit shedding a pleasantly blended cascade of pinks and reds and golds. Wayna's neighbors had piled Yungun poles into a rough bench beneath its branches. Unique sat and gestured to her; she sank beside him gratefully. Always so tired.

He possessed himself of both her hands but kept his head lowered, eyes averted. "My dear. You're dying."

"You— What— Unique? What's that mean? Unique?"

He peeked up at her, held her gaze, dropped it after a moment. "You're dying," he repeated. "The Handaglory. It's poison. It's poisoning you." He looked up again. "I'm sorry."

"You can't—you're sure?" He said something back. Fear made everything but itself hard to feel, see, hear—like cold oil covering her eyes, filling her ears. She shivered.

Concentrate. What had he said? What was true?

Wayna was dying. A gradual death. Like the seeds of the wild potato. Nothing to do with the pain her download gave. It could happen to anyone who ate hardly anything else but Handaglory. As she'd been doing.

Her fatigue was actually the onset of paralysis.

Trill—

"But if I stop, I'll get better, won't I?"

"Maybe. We'll have to give it a try."

She pulled her hands away from his too-tight grip. "You don't think—"

"I don't know!" Unique shouted. "I don't know! Without equipment—records—references—" He was standing, hauling her up, shaking her, then shoving her away to shout more. "I don't know! I don't fucking—" He stopped midsentence and sat back down. "Sorry. Sorry."

"We'll ask Dr. Ops for another download for me." He'd turned her down before, though. Said there was a rule. Unique shook his head, lowered his heavy eyebrows.

"We'll ask," she repeated. Wayna was amazed at how calm she sounded. The thick coating of fear helped. And the tiredness made excitement too much work. The paralysis.

Now a number of doorways had heads and lights sticking out of them. People wondering what had made Unique yell. Here came Jawann. He'd be sorry he was right about whether Wayna should have stopped testing. Jawann.

Robeson. Unique. Trill. Trill.

More buoyant than *Psyche Moth's* training pool, the body of water clients called the High Seas lifted Carpenter Marie and her four fellow trustees above itself with every stroke they swam. Their uniforms had sealed at wrist and ankle, holding in air that helped them float. Behind them they towed the lander in five sections, boat-like shells holding their supplies: beacon, food, rechargeable batteries. Not a lot. Just enough to set them apart. Just enough to make life a little easier for them compared to for the regular prisoners.

Carpenter Marie closed her eyes as the stinging spray blew into her face. Virches were lousy at conveying these sorts of details; she composed and stored a note to Dr. Ops recommending goggles for the next round of volunteers. Her promised direct access would have to wait for the beacon setup; even then, it would only be good during certain hours of the ship's orbit.

Blinking hard, she oriented herself to the blur of the coast. No marine megafauna on this part of Amends from what they knew. She did her best not to worry about being eaten. Anyway, they were nearly there.

The weights they'd worn on *Psyche Moth* had helped build up her muscles; her arms and legs ached, though, by the time she and the others staggered up the steep slope of the pebbly beach. A brightly colored flock of winged animals—prettybirds, the clients had named them—swooped around them a moment, then disappeared over the bluffs to the west.

They set off to make camp up on those bluffs, despite Carpenter Marie's muted protests at the climb. Amends's tides were gentle; they'd be perfectly fine sleeping at sea level. But as Tembo pointed out, weather was always chaotic, and there were temporary systems present in this hemisphere that could compromise their safety.

So they left the lander sections behind and carried half their contents around a long mound of what looked like dead roots and weathered tree limbs. On the mound's far side, a ramp of loose stone spilled from the bluffs' top. That was where they went up, since it was easy. On closer inspection, Carpenter Marie suspected the pile of tangled "wood" was this world's equivalent of a jumble of skeletons. The shapes were familiar: protruding knobs, socket-like junctions, flanged cradles and gently curving ridges. Back on board *Psyche Moth*, she'd studied Amends's fauna instead of doing relax virches, focusing heavily on this hemisphere.

But she didn't say anything about her theory. Bree and Butterfly and Cheekbones had been taking their lead from Tembo since Dr. Ops gave them their assignments, and when Carpenter Marie was added she'd decided to go along with the group for the time being. She would assert herself later.

A fairly flat open area lay just over the bluffs' crumbling edge—not for several meters did the brush and woods start, and even then a wide swathe of an ankle-high fuzzy growth split it like a highway. Tembo said the panoramic view up here would warn them of any attacks. They could see the distant settlement clearly. Carpenter Marie couldn't find fault with that. Besides, the bluff's surface was softer, she thought, spreading her tent bag. She picked a spot as far away from Tembo and Cheekbones as she could get and still be in sight of Butterfly and Bree, the other two women. That put her right against the base of the area's one freestanding boulder, which probably saved her life.

Dreaming in her meat of an avalanche from a virch she'd done long ago, back on Earth, she woke lying on rumbling, rolling ground. Confusion filled her—was what she felt real? She jerked into sitting position. She pushed back the stiffened shelter over her head and by the dim light of the leaves surrounding it saw a huge, incomprehensible shadow rushing along the "highway" toward camp. She didn't know why that frightened her. "Tembo! Butterfly! Bree!"

Their yells back were hard to hear over the rising noise of what—Thunder? Volcanoes? Like a low cloud speeding nearer, nearer, second by second, a crashing roar bore down on her. She ducked behind her rock. Drowning screams mixed with the awful pounding sound—hundreds, thousands of hooves hitting the soil and stone, and no, yes, the others, smashing them. Their dying cries vanished in heaving darkness.

Animals. An enormous herd of animals running by. That's what this was. Flashing eyes and heaving flanks showed in the fading light of torn leaves caught on their erect quills. Grazers, stampeding through the broken dark.

Nothing but the bluff's edge in the direction they were headed. They reached it and went over bellowing. Fell bellowing through the air. Helpless with rage and pain. Crashing at the bottom onto the pile of their old bones.

Then silence. Nothing disturbed the sudden quiet but the whistles and chirps of a passing flock of prettybirds.

Dust and silence. Carpenter Marie dared to move from her boulder's shelter. She sloughed off the tent bag and took a step. Two steps. Stopped and stood still, listening. Silence. No sobs. No groans. No moans for help.

Dust and another smell. A blend of shit and blood.

The nearest had been Bree. She should make sure there was nothing she could do. Go see. The dust was settling, but the dim light grew quickly dimmer. She walked as slowly as she could to where she thought she remembered Bree lying down. As soon as Carpenter Marie saw the dark smear that was left of the other woman on the pale dirt she was done.

Past the boulder in the other direction, the open ground continued. The leaves faded as the night wore on. Carpenter Marie kept going that way as long as she could see. Longer, actually—once she'd become completely blind she crawled. She only gave up on that after putting a hand forward and finding nothingness. The bluffs' edge. She'd probably come far enough away from the camp anyway.

She curled up, wrapping her arms around herself for comfort. The black air was cold. She'd left the tent bag behind. But she'd reach Jubilee tomorrow. Today. The clients would come back with her to bring the things they'd left—she'd left—they'd left with the lander sections. And whatever was salvageable from the camp. And bury the rest.

Dr. Ops didn't keep copies. She'd asked him during her interview, when they talked about the danger.

Well before dawn the bushes and other flowering plants began to shine red and pink and yellow and blue. Pretty, and it showed Carpenter Marie where to go. By the time the sky itself was bright she'd reached the settlement.

⟡

Wayna wanted to *do* something. She couldn't. She was dying, and that was all. She tried her best not to cling to Trill, not to change anything in the routine of his life. He'd grow up without her. Maybe he'd forget her, never miss her. Maybe that was best.

Jawann and Robeson took turns sitting with her, which both comforted and annoyed her. Today she waited to struggle out of her hammock on her own till everyone else was busy—Robeson taking Trill with her to the Care Dopkwe's gathering on the sandy beach; Jawann just a house away, helping Scrapple grind rocks for her experimental glazes. He'd told Wayna five times he would come if she called. She'd rather not have to.

She forced her legs and back straight. Piss made her bladder ache to be emptied. Trill's night jar in the corner was further than it seemed, further away than yesterday somehow. But she made it and sighed in heartfelt relief as the stream of urine splashed and pooled in the clay container. It made a tuneful melody. How many more mornings would she hear it?

Two weeks since Unique told Wayna she'd poisoned herself. No treatment helped. Her strength diminished constantly, continuously. It ran out of her like water.

Wayna wiped clean with her cloth, placed it in the laundry basket. Wrapped herself in a sheet of fabric patched together from worn-out overalls—it was easy to put on and take off.

She shuffled over to the soft heap of rags and fuzz her wife and husband had assembled for her to rest on. Better when she didn't try lifting her feet.

Her mind wasn't tired like her body. Sad, yes. But you could only cry so much.

She picked up the thread of her current project: curtains for the house's doorway. The thinnest strands of the tenderest, youngest red vines had been hung from one of the house's rafters. Between them Wayna was weaving a loose, netlike structure—see-through, but enough of a presence to inform visitors they'd come to a boundary, to put them in mind of the house's inhabitants' privacy. She had already completed the upper reaches, which was good. Standing a long time was hard now. Seated, she could reach high enough to work on the bottom row.

"Hey." Brownie walked in without scratching politely at the doorframe. "Ain't seen you lately."

On general principles no one had told Jubilee's five remaining trustees about Wayna's poisoning. The less they knew.

"Yeah, Unique says I gotta get over myself. Menstrual cramps and bloating ain't a serious threat to life," Wayna began, skirting around the lie they'd agreed on, coming as close to it as her ethics allowed. She rested her arms on her knees. "And—"

Brownie interrupted her. "Wanted you to hear the news soon as I saw her. There a new trustee come from *Psyche Moth*."

Wayna frowned. "Only one?" Brownie had boasted earlier about the number of trustees posted here doubling. Ten trustees would have been half the amount they'd had when they landed, but still more than anyone wanted to deal with.

"They was five of em. Grazers gone and killed four."

"But I thought trustees were supposed to know better—didn't Dr. Ops train them about what to avoid down here?"

"Woman says they was a stampede. No way *to* avoid em. Sundiata claim all the meat gone by the time he and Twyla got back where it happen."

She had heard about Grazer stampedes. Never seen one, but the evidence—the heaps of bones at the feet of different cliffs—pointed to their past frequency. What caused them? One more thing to investigate. No good ideas yet—

There was a price for letting her attention wander: heavy and hard, Brownie's left hand landed suddenly on Wayna's thigh. She shifted the sheet to cover that area, which made him lift it momentarily. When he put it back it was higher. Almost up to her groin. He looked at her out of the corner of his blue-green eyes.

Dropping her glance to his crotch, Wayna considered what to do now he'd gone this far. A faint stirring against the tightness of his overalls and the acrid scent of arousal let her know he felt her gaze. Was it worth keeping him on the hook so they could reel him in whenever they wanted to know what Dr. Ops was up to? Jubilee's prisoners had learned a lot from the man, and they'd never let him in on any really important secrets.

How bad could it be? How long could it last?

How long did she have, though?

Turning her head to look down at his hand on her lap, Wayna licked her lips and cleared her throat. She wished she wasn't hesitating. She had wanted to do something. Here something was.

"You like me, Wayna? I like you." As if he were some little player hanging at the mall. Rather than lie, she clasped his hand between her own, carried it to her mouth, and kissed it. Bringing its back to face her, she breathed softly on the sensitive valleys between the trustee's tanned and calloused fingers. Then darted her tongue to touch the white skin there, tasting its dried sweat. An audible gasp rewarded her. She pressed her left hand against the outline of the trustee's swelling cock, swiveled his hand to rest horizontally on her right, and nipped lightly at the knuckles of the index. Swallowed the whole of the long middle finger, scraping her teeth along its edges, laving them with soothing moisture afterwards, sucking and swirling, withdrawing the finger to pay minute attention to the pad of flesh below it, trailing down from there to the protected cup of his palm—

"Oh! Sorry!" A strange woman stood in the doorway. "Jawann said—never mind. Sorry. I can come back later—" She had on crisp, black-and-grey overalls: the new trustee.

Beside Wayna, Brownie stiffened and went limp at the same time. "No no no!" he said. "Don't go—please! I was just tellin Wayna here all about you. She a model prisoner—coulda been one of us, probally." He jumped to his feet. "Come on in an meet her."

"Now?" The woman was visibly skeptical.

"Why not? Sure thing—Wayna, this Carpenter Marie, fresh down from *Psyche Moth*."

"And you Wayna? Jawann said, but—you *the* Wayna? The one who design them emergency shelter packs for Singa-Poor?"

"Uh, yeah." Part of her life as a "terrorist." Prisoners didn't usually ask each other about what they'd done before getting sent to Amends. Either you knew or you didn't.

"Sweetness!" Though she'd been standing poised to depart on the threshold, the woman—Carpenter Marie—came all the way in. "I was hopin to meet you." She took Brownie's seat and curled her hands into awkward fists underneath her prominent collarbone.

"Me? Why me?"

"We used them shelter packs in Vancouver, joined em up together to make our clinic. Did you know—"

Now it was Brownie who stood in the doorway. "Jawann, how you doin?"

Her husband's voice sounded coolish. "I'm doin." His face was blank as he came in. He thought they should have found a way by now to kill all the trustees without arousing Dr. Ops's suspicion.

He smiled briefly and was perfectly polite as Wayna introduced him to Carpenter Marie. He asked the guest if she wanted some water to drink. But after she and Brownie left he didn't say anything. For a long while. He lay silently in his hammock; if she hadn't seen that his eyes were open, Wayna wouldn't have known he was awake.

Robeson came home with Trill asleep in her arms. Jawann got up to kiss and hug them. He brought the boy over to Wayna, then laid him in his daddy's hammock. Wayna's wife settled next to her on her narrow mattress, tugging her down till her head rested cradled between Robeson's crossed legs. Smoothing Wayna's hair back from her forehead, she asked, "You feelin any better, mama?" She looked up to Jawann, hovering over their son. "You think she gettin better?"

"No." He hunkered down on the floor opposite them, back propped against their roof's central pillar. "She worse. Right, Wayna?"

She sighed. "Right." As Unique had said. Slow degeneration. Without a cure.

"You got no time to waste on fools like Brownie."

Robeson's fingers stopped moving. "Jawann?"

He heaved himself to stand, covered his face with both hands, then pulled them away. "I came in, I could *smell* it. Wayna, tell me he ain't been gettin on you."

She never told anything but the truth. She kept quiet.

"I will kill him. I will kill him," Robeson repeated tonelessly. "I will —"

"The pact! You can't—" Once Dr. Ops found out they were straight out killing trustees, Jubilee—all the settlements—would be destroyed and her fellow prisoners hunted down. A few might escape. "Robeson, no!"

"Ain't any kinda use bein jealous," said Jawann.

"I know! I know! Don't tell me that—tell me what *is* any use! Tell me what to do!" Robeson was yelling now. Much less scary.

Jawann must have thought the same. He argued back. "I ain't know *that*! You have a way to keep Wayna outta Brownie sight? So he won't mess with her? She can't be goin Gatherin no more."

The noise woke up Trill, set him crying. That put an end to that fight. Wayna watched wearily as Jawann fed him crushed and stewed rosetoo cereal. More than their son's share—hers, too. Wayna didn't need to eat as much these days. Watching her son and husband, she drifted to sleep and dreamed the answer to their biggest problem.

If they hadn't decided to try moving her she might have forgotten the solution, let it drown in the murky waters of her other dreams.

Robeson had her arms under Wayna's pointless knees; her red hair shone a weird, dark maroon beneath the branch of the Hannakka bush dangling from the roof.

Jawann carried Wayna's upper body, which was still marginally effective. She twisted her head to tell him her idea.

"Aw, *hell* no!"

"But it'll work," she insisted. "The poison's cumulative—a meal or two won't hurt you and Robeson. And I'm dying anyway." She made them sit her back upright, made them listen while she explained what she needed them to do. Made them agree.

"So you pregnant again?" Brownie asked.

Carpenter Marie made a face at the rudeness of his question. But Wayna didn't seem offended by it.

"Yeah. I weaned Trill a while ago. It's only natural."

Wayna's husband Jawann held out a stew dish of the peppery-flavored roots they called Handaglory. "Want some more? We got plenty. Thanks to you all." He scooped a ladleful onto her plate without waiting for an answer, then divided the rest between the other five trustees seated outside the hut with her.

"Ain't no thing," said Sundiata, their senior. He wore the overalls on his short, muscular download unfastened to his waist. "You gonna have to tell the rest a Jubilee about a new food eventually, but for now we just help you keep this on the —"

"You don't *look* pregnant," Brownie persisted. Carpenter Marie wanted to hit him. But that wouldn't look good in front of the prisoners. The clients.

"We tryna fatten her up." Jawann picked up a pitcher and poured a thick liquid into Brownie's mug, then offered it to Carpenter Marie. She had already drained her own mug empty once. She couldn't bring herself to turn down seconds, though; the drink was sweet and milkily delicious, the texture reminiscent of a shake, the taste of cold chai.

Some part of her was suspicious. These clients' discovery of such a versatile new staple, simultaneously with the unexpected depletion of the trustees' dedicated stocks of luxury foods — that couldn't be coincidence, could it? Yet the prisoners ate with them.

Robeson, the woman who was either Jawann's lover or his second wife, came out of the hut's door bearing a bowl of green leaves. "Here's the salad — I hope you saved room." Next to Carpenter Marie the smallest trustee, Twyla, groaned.

Though they were rivals — they had to be, it was only human nature — relations between the two females certainly seemed friendly: Wayna got the first serving of Robeson's salad, and before returning inside Robeson stooped to tenderly rearrange her pillows.

All six trustees left with baskets of Handaglory roots and leaves, secret supplements to the rations they were restricted to with the rest of the settlement. Their bribes. Brownie did his best to make Wayna promise she'd come cook his. He gave up when Jawann got them laughing at his imitation of her vomiting all over her preparations.

Carpenter Marie waited till she and the other trustees were more than half the way back to their quarters before she mentioned missing her utility knife. Twyla offered to go with her to retrieve it but didn't insist when Carpenter Marie turned the offer down.

She had so far been unable to spend the time with Wayna she had hoped for when she picked her assignment. Forgetting her utility knife hadn't exactly been an accident.

Jubilee's market was shutting down, the leaves tied to its light poles fading like their living counterparts in the woods and brush beyond. Carpenter Marie noted a couple of women cutting their eyes at her as she passed them by. Slowing down for a closer look she saw a lumpy shape toward the back of their booth. The cloth covering it—too casually tossed in place—showed the dull glint of forbidden metal. She should check, but it was very likely shovels or something else nonviolent. Nothing Dr. Ops would punish anyone over.

Besides, she had somewhere else to be.

She swung around the corner and onto the street where Wayna lived. A tiny child, barely able to walk on its own, ran away from her and into the embrace of a crouching man. She nodded at him but didn't stop to speak.

Strangely, though the night's darkness had become almost full, Wayna had stayed outside her hut, sprawled on her pillows.

She held the utility knife, playing with its release, running her nails along its sharp edge.

"Careful!" Carpenter Marie called out. The woman gave an odd half-jump from the hips up and peered unseeingly in her direction.

Carpenter Marie stepped into the light spilling through the hut's crudely curtained doorway. "Glad it was you found that," she said. "I woulda worried with some people. Mighta had to file a report. Mighta had it disappear on me." She held out her hand.

"Doesn't this set-up bother you?" Wayna asked. She didn't give her the knife.

Carpenter Marie knelt in front of her. "What gonna bother me?" But she knew. "Like how I can have somethin you can't?"

"Well, look who's got it now." But Wayna leaned forward and put the knife on the ground between them.

Carpenter Marie left it there. "Everyone have their own advantage over everyone else." Brains. Creativity, like she worshiped in Wayna. Beauty, like she'd had in her old body.

"Yeah, but I didn't get my advantage from Dr. Ops."

"Come on. We all get everything from Dr. Ops round here."

"Then I didn't give him anything in return to get it."

This wasn't the conversation Carpenter Marie had imagined.

"You ever think about that, Carpenter Marie? What you give up so you can be a trustee?"

"Sure." She shrugged. Everything on the application waiver—the full-access implant, everything. How else was she supposed to take care of herself, though? Not a real question. She knew the answer. No way else.

But there were things she actually didn't know, like where she could get such wonderful ideas as Wayna had. And how she could make people help her put them out in the world. And why Wayna hadn't ever given up on changing what was awful but inevitable about life. And more. Carpenter Marie's secret, unasked questions throbbed in the air. They were the reason she'd signed up for this job, the reason she'd picked this posting to Jubilee. The reason she'd slipped the knife from her pocket and kicked it under her mat.

Her real questions. Choose one, any one, she commanded herself, but it was Wayna who broke the silence. "Where'd you come up with the name 'Carpenter Marie'? That what you used to do? Carpentry? That why you liked them shelters?"

"It was for a band. The Carpenters. Mama liked em. And Marie was her dead sister's middle name." She had never told anyone besides Wayna that second part.

Moisture fell on her bare wrist. For a moment Carpenter Marie thought she was crying. But it was only rain, light, a sprinkle.

The knife would rust. She wiped it off on the leg of her overalls and put it in her pocket.

Jawann came out, pushing the flimsy curtain aside. He eyed Carpenter Marie for a moment, but then turned to stoop over his wife. "You ready to come to bed, mama?" His voice was low, quiet, but full of emotion. Longing. Lust. Love.

"I guess." Wayna apologized to Carpenter Marie as Jawann lifted her up. "I get so tired these days." Because of her pregnancy, she must mean.

Carpenter Marie stood, too, while Jawann shifted Wayna in his arms so her head lay against his shoulder. And kissed her. That was Carpenter Marie's cue. She tried to step away unobtrusively, but Wayna stopped her. "Wait."

She returned to the patch of light. Above her arched the great night, where soon *Psyche Moth* would fly into range. When she would report to Dr. Ops how well the settlement did. Very well. How they'd even found a brand new food source they were sharing.

"Will you come back tomorrow? For lunch?"

Carpenter Marie tried to sound casual. More time with Wayna. "All right. If you want."

"You into that drink thing, aintcha?" Jawann asked her. He had noticed. That was nice. She nodded.

"I can't be here. Gotta get up early to go huntin prettybird eggs for the day, but I promise I make a big batch of it in the mornin so you get as much as you want. And you gonna be one a the first to sample this new spread we cookin up outta Handaglory roots an rollin in they leaves. We plannin on puttin together enough a those to see how long they keep. Bring em back to quarters with you. Take all you can carry."

It was a nice speech, but Jawann kept looking away from her during it, kept lowering his gaze almost surreptitiously to his wife's face. Watchfully. Obsessively. As if she'd disappear if he wasn't careful.

Once more, Carpenter Marie left.

Once more, she came back.

This time the hut's lights were out. Voices came from inside. She recognized Wayna's, though it seemed thicker than earlier — was that a sob? — but couldn't figure out what she was saying. Jawann's reply was clear enough: "—if she do, so what? You been knowin you hafta pay a price, too. What you expect."

Then sighs, moans. No more words.

"*...you hafta pay a price, too.*" What did that mean? Carpenter Marie walked home alone, ignoring her fast-becoming-familiar surroundings, mind on this latest puzzle.

Another question. Maybe tomorrow she'd have the courage to ask it. Tomorrow or someday soon.

In Colors Everywhere

*Clients must not be killed. WestHem has opted
to destroy their original bodies while preserving
psychoemotional components. Transport to
Amends completes the allotted punishment, taking
into consideration the impossibility of return to
Earth, along with the harsh experiences certain
to arise from atechnical living conditions. On this
account, however, minimal attempts should be
made to ameliorate these conditions.*
— Mission Guidelines, *Psyche Moth*, 2055

TRILL WALKED HOME through the Rainshadow Mountains with Adia, her former mentor. Not alone.

The sky had been high all day. Now, with evening, it came low, wetting them and their surroundings with mist. Silver beaded the fuzz beneath their feet.

Adia was tough, though an elder. She walked steadily, without complaint. She ought to have been tired even before they started; she and Trill had spent the week teaching a cohort of tens-to-thirteens how to weave buildings.

Jubilee, the largest settlement of prisoners on Amends for two generations now, had decided to bud a new village. As expected, the tens-to-thirteens were eager for adventure, the fourteens-to-seventeens hardly less so. The site they chose, where the peninsula joined the mainland's western coast, fronted a beach on Unrest Bay, quieter waters than Jubilee's open ocean. "Unrest" might well be picked as the new place's name; the selection would be finalized by those who ended up living there.

The first wave had big plans. They would build boats and fish there, these two age-groups claimed. They'd start double the Fisher Dopkwes and beat the older settlement's harvest. The eighteens-to-twenty-fours were of course more skeptical, having just discovered cynicism. The few twenty-fives-to-forty-fives — Trill's age cohort — who had chosen to emigrate with them smiled and nodded encouragingly whenever the idea came up. And then returned to the work of their current dopkwes: rope spinning, planting, preserving, and so on.

Trill and Adia had left to go home late that morning with no urgency. No Rogues or Solitaries had been sighted in the area for months. And it was summer; even when the sky came down to kiss them they were sure that leaflight would last long enough for their trip. They'd eaten a big lunch at the halfway point, so they wouldn't be hungry till they arrived —

Trill stopped before she knew why. Adia, ahead of her, kept walking moments after the sound became audible to Trill: a scream, a shriek sinking lower, louder — closer, Trill realized. She shrank to crouch under a dripping Chrismas tree while looking up, frightened but curious. Like a tooth or a knife, the sound bit through the air. A flock of prettybirds burst out of a fall of redvines hanging from a bluff and flew south. The sound grew, grew, the rising roar of someone who never needed a new breath.

Adia still stood in the open, face tilted up as if she could see the screaming. Trill staggered to her feet to coax the Lady who had trained her to shelter, to safety.

BOOM!

On her hands and knees, Trill looked around. Nothing had changed — except that she had to piss from fear. But Adia stood stubbornly upright in the same place, on the same rough path just beginning to be worn between Jubilee and the new settlement. She stood calmly, relaxed, as if facing nothing more serious than a test — though she'd become a Lady decades ago. As though nothing threatened her.

The elder shook her head and glanced at Trill over her shoulder, then came to help her rise. "Long time since I heard anything like that." Adia's words were soft as whispers. Why? "Poor shang. You got no clue, do you? That come from Dr. Ops."

Trill stepped back off the path to release her water. She whispered too. "From *Psyche Moth*?" Her clothes didn't rustle. Her water made no sound striking the fuzz.

"What? Speak up!"

"Dr. Ops on the *Psyche Moth*?" Trill shouted. She understood now. Adia wasn't whispering, so she didn't have to. It was just that the huge noise had made it hard to hear anything else afterwards.

"He the one. It ain't a bomb or nothin — mission guidelines say he ain't spozed to kill us. Naw, he just sent us another drone, sounded like. First since I had my final period. I wish I coulda seen it. Fuckin Chrismas trees in the way. Wonder what kinda trouble he put inside it?"

❧

Low intrusion surveillance recommended. High-orbit monitoring to be supplemented by trustee insertion at periodic intervals keyed to instructions relayed from verified WestHem government facilities via translight. If no such instructions are received for over 20 years, refer to procedures for establishing surface stock.

— Mission Guidelines, *Psyche Moth*, 2055

ᴥ

Trill was working out a design when they sent for her, an idea about something to help the Hunters Dopkwe that had come from talking with her ex-lover Hett, LeeRai's father. It was a sort of a box that became a basket when its walls dried out. A strap over the forehead and the high-climbing sixes-to-nines could pack one of them as full of phibian eggs as they liked. Hang the box-baskets from a line, and even with the lids left on, there'd be enough air getting inside to cure the leathery eggs slowly, the way she liked them.

"Lady?"

Trill looked up from her workbasin. Dola, an eighteens-to-twenty-fours identifying as female, leaned tentatively in at the shed's entrance. "Will you come with me to the baths?"

A summons. Trill nodded. "Just let me—" She did what she needed to without further explanation: tied off her project's last side panel, laid it on a rack, emptied her workbasin's water into the shop's barrel, and wiped dry her hands.

Outside, the sky had mellowed to a gold like beer. Evening. She should have stopped work long ago to visit the kitchen for food. There would always be something, though. More tempting was the urge to find the fives-and-unders before they went to sleep. She hadn't spent the night with LeeRai since coming home four days—almost a full week—ago.

That morning they had raced each other on the hard-packed sand of the beach. Trill had laughed, the breath hot and easy in her lungs, her daughter big and plump and bronzed by the sky. And getting so strong! So fast! Always moving—it would be strange and lovely to see her lying still, asleep—

But the other Ladies wanted her now.

She followed Dola up the hill. This neighborhood of Jubilee, up against the Rainshadows, had drawn people to it from the settlement's main site because of the hot springs. As they walked the sun disappeared, ducking behind the mountains, though the sky's grace and the leaves' first radiance provided plenty of light.

Dola had applied to become a Lady that spring, shortly after conscripting Trill to help the Gardeners Dopkwe. Having recently completed her entry trials, she was now an apprentice, in training for her final test. Many Ladies were part of the Gardeners Dopkwe, since plant lore was intimately tied to their power.

Trill didn't mind helping Inker, Dola's main mentor. She liked the girl. They had sung together while working and since then, too. The eighteens-to-twenty-fours had a good voice and knew all the verses to "Billie Jean." She wore her hair in bunches of thin braids braided together into three thicker ones these days, the same as Trill did. Around her neck hung a necklace woven of redvine tendrils, one of those things Trill made when she had nothing else to keep her busy.

They climbed a fuzz-covered slope and descended into a shallow, wooded valley. Steam rose from the dark water pooled at its center. Around the water's edge several of the Jubilee Ladies lounged. In the leaves' glow Trill saw Adia's sharp-chinned face; the elder next to her, braiding her long, white hair, was Robeson, Adia's friend. She recognized others, too, such as Kala and True, also from Trill's cohort. On Earth, the groups the Ladies modeled themselves after wouldn't have considered admitting Trill, Kala, or True, let alone an applicant Dola's age. But the empty clone bodies given to the first prisoners had all been twenty-fives-to-forty-fives. "You don't have to be old to be wise," they said. That was why the younger cohorts were welcome to at least ask to belong.

One person in the pool wasn't a Lady. Standing in the middle of the spring was an unfamiliar eighteens-to-twenty-fours—from another settlement? She didn't know everyone here; Jubilee was home to almost 32,000 people. If not for the Ladies there would have been twice that number—too many to prosper.

She folded her dress and underwear and left them on a bench. The dark water washed warmly over her feet, calves, knees—

"Stop." Trill obeyed. The voice was Robeson's; she held the bright, dying branch of a Hannakka bush, meaning she was the Ladies' speaker for now. "Don't need to stand no deeper. You ain't makin no report; we got Adia's. And Odell's. We called you for a different reason. Work."

"Work?"

"We want you to go where that thing Dr. Ops sent landed."

The Ladies had used her before for duties not obviously connected with her dopkwe, of course. After her test, when she became one of them, they told Trill that honesty was her particular power; lies made her weak. Because since then she'd told the truth scrupulously, paying almost obsessive attention to conveying details, she was their best reporter. But— "But— but—where? Where is it? How do you know?"

"Odell a trader comin here from Hamza. Six of em together on the road an they think it dropped down between where they camped at and us. They was gonna radio—" Eefay, to the far south, had supplied Hamza, Jubilee, and the nine other settlements on Amends with crystal sets. "—but that didn't seem real safe. *Psyche Moth* mighta changed orbit. Dr. Ops mighta heard. They split up instead."

"You want me to go with—" Odell wore no clothing, which meant Trill had no way of telling if the stranger was a him or a her. "You want us to go together and find out…what?"

Adia put her hand over Robeson's tiny one, sharing the speaker's branch with her. "What kinda trouble he put inside," she said, echoing the words she'd spoken on the path from the new place.

Dola would go too, with Trill as her mentor. Training. It made sense. The girl was due for her final test soon. She needed fieldwork, a task to take her outside the settlement.

Trill acknowledged to herself that she'd rather stay home and weave. The men and women in her dopkwe had interesting ideas that kept them talking some nights long after the last leaves faded. But she waded out of the water and dressed again without protest. The three of them would depart at flowerlight. She had just a short time to eat and sleep.

❦

> *Offspring produced by clients during their sentences have committed no crimes but must serve with them, as they are likely to be contaminated with clients' views. Under no circumstances are they to be allowed to develop extraplanetary capabilities. Similar caution must be exercised regarding any later generations coming into direct contact with clients.*
> —Mission Guidelines, *Psyche Moth*, 2055

Trill woke as the flowers' buds were barely beginning to unfurl. Beside her, Odell stirred gently, driven from sleep's depths by the growing light. Their sex had been excellent. According to his estimate—Odell was currently male, and apparently had been since the age of six—the stretch of shoreline they now neared was close to the waters where whatever Dr. Ops sent must have come down.

She sat up, twisting, lifting one buttock and then the other to free her dress, and pulled it on over her head. "Dola!"

"Yes, Lady!" The eighteens-to-twenty-fours girl had climbed a bottle tree like a much younger person. "Is it time for breakfast?"

"Come and find out."

Odell rose and left silently to relieve himself. Dola descended and did likewise, then returned to eat the tofruit they had brought as provisions for their trip. Tasteless but somehow more satisfying than ordinary garden crops, tofruit grew from seeds that had arrived on Amends years ago in a drone sent to Nunavut Island. So Dola said.

Trill went a little ways off to make her own water and earth. She buried them quickly, yet Dola had again climbed a tall tree when she got back. For a member of the Gardeners Dopkwe she spent very little time on the ground. "What are you searching for up there?"

The bottle tree's leaves shivered as Dola scrambled down to the forest floor. "A flock of prettybirds. They were looking at us while you slept. Then they flew away."

Odell frowned and pushed the blond fronds of his hair back from his temples. "Anything else? Smoke or — or glints of metal? Or is some part of the ocean an unusual color?"

"No."

Not till noon did they come upon a sign of Dr. Ops's intrusion: trustees talking loud enough they could be heard ten arms away. Two of them. At first Trill thought they were Rogues, though none had been reported north of Hamza. But they were arguing about what Dr. Ops wanted like they knew. According to the elders, he told trustees his secrets.

"How come you ain't let us start with that other place, the closer one? Coulda got clients carryin our equipment. Be quicker than us havin to lug evvathing, an we spozed —"

A high, decisive voice cut the other off. "Dr. Ops sent us here to take care a business, not be goin all over, back an forth.

118

We start up in Jubilee, get clients there to help us an head on south, we be fine. Like I said yesterday, an the day before. Like we already *doin*. Now stop askin me am I sure."

Both spoke the way many elders did, so they, too, must have originally occupied black bodies.

Trill, Dola, and Odell stepped softly to within three arms of the pair. She saw the strangers through the day-dull leaves: both men, judging by their overalls, with the pale skin of babies. They faced each other over four stacks of four smooth grey-and-black boxes. She edged closer and one box lit up like a tiny, square Chrismas tree. The men fell suddenly silent. After a long while the high-voiced one called out that he could see them, then contradicted himself by asking them to show themselves.

Odell emerged into the open from behind Trill.

"Come on. Where's the other two?"

Trill was impressed. Adia's claims of accuracy for Dr. Ops's tracking equipment held up. Could his weapons kill as horribly as she and Robeson said? The hand of one man now held something. Without waiting to learn what, Trill followed Odell. So did Dola.

"Well. That's much better. Have a seat." The high-voiced man gestured at the fuzz to one side of the stacks with what Trill assumed was a weapon. "We trustees come from the *Psyche Moth*. Been waitin here for you — you stay in Jubilee?"

Trill nodded. "Me and Dola do; Odell here belongs in Hamza."

"Well, I'm Isabelle and this is Freddie. Dr. Ops figured you could use a more permanent installation at this point, so he picked us to set one up. After we take care a Jubilee we can help the other settlements."

Did the man think they were stupid? "Take care of us how?"

Isabelle patted the top of one of the stacks. "With the latest advances in knowledge just come from Earth, transmissions got sent to us only a few years back. These here banks contain blueprints — um, that mean models, plans —"

Trill tried to look as ignorant as Isabelle obviously believed she was.

"— for improvements, medicines, time-saving devices —"

"Of course, only Isabelle and I be able to access things for you," Freddie added. Maybe he was afraid he'd be murdered if he didn't make that plain.

What the trustees *said* they wanted in exchange for their "improvements" was safe conduct to Jubilee. They *said* they were worried about Rogues and Solitaries. Which made no sense; they'd been fine for the week-and-a-half since Trill heard them arrive, and they'd just demonstrated they could tell when someone approached their camp. And Isabelle carried a weapon.... Again Trill pretended like she had no mind.

Going along with the lie about Rogues and Solitaries though none were known to be nearby, the three took turns "scouting." This consisted of getting far enough away that they no longer registered on the trustees' tracking instruments and then spying on what they said and did.

Sixteen boxes. Either Freddie or Isabelle stayed with their "equipment" at all times. Trill's attempts to wander off aimlessly with the four boxes she carried mostly failed. Twice she managed to open a box's latched drawer to reveal mysterious black slabs of identical lightweight material: plastic, like a lot of things the Scavengers Dopkwe in Dinetah used and traded. The second time, Isabelle caught her, and she pretended it had been an accident. The last time.

At night, the sky showed them *Psyche Moth's* orbit. It hadn't changed. They calculated when it would most likely fly overhead; that was when Freddie and Isabelle could learn their "guides'" locations easily from Dr. Ops. That was when the prisoners took care to be where expected.

Climbing trees in pursuit of prettybirds, Dola discovered that above the height of seven arms she was undetectable. Trill in her underwear was almost as agile as the eighteens-to-twenty-fours girl. One afternoon, the trustees thought they were completely alone. Stretched out on a branch—almost within eyesight, if they'd bothered to look for her—Trill listened closely.

Freddie was grumbling about having to walk. Elders reminisced about easier ways of traveling, too. And faster ones. "We takin so *long*," he complained. It had only been five days—just a week. "We know where Jubilee is—cain't we do the job right here?"

"You wanna set up equipment an tear it down again inna middle a nowhere on the chance one a these the best bet? An explain that to em how? Look, Dr. Ops say do one in every settlement. So we go to Jubilee. With the clients we with. Then we probably have a lot more success gettin a big bunch of em to buy what we sayin."

"Awright." But Freddie wasn't through complaining. "Still wish they'd hurry up. Or we had a auto, hover, *somethin*. Ain't it spozed to be more sunshine when we get there? So tired a these goddam fuck-ass clouds an this mothafuckin fog I could strangle the shit—"

Despite the danger—or maybe because of it—Trill laughed so hard she fell ten arms to the ground. Cursing the *sky*? What good was that going to do? The sky was *there*, always would be.

She lay giggling on the fuzz, unhurt. Good thing Chrismas tree branches were so thick and soft.

But here came the two trustees thrashing through the Hannakka bushes—of course they'd heard her crashing down. Trill crawled away and "returned" to their camp by another route. She called them back there and told a tale of chasing off a dangerous Rogue from the spot where she'd fallen.

❧

Given a timelag for Earth-Amends communications of nearly a decade, and a minimum duration of almost a century for any physical return trip, rehabilitation efforts made after clients are settled should consist of observation and counseling only. None will have even the slightest effect on WestHem paradigms. Natural tendencies as embedded in the provided genetic material will eventually assert themselves.
— Mission Guidelines, *Psyche Moth*, 2055

They arrived at the new settlement as the sun was about to rise over the Rainshadows. New gardens lined the rough path, rosetoo blooms shining their last yellows, reds, blues, and shocking pinks. They passed the two eighteens-to-twenty-fours on perimeter watch without either of the trustees noticing them. Trill had sent word ahead about their arrival via Dola. They were expected.

The two houses Trill and Adia had helped the emigrants start were fully woven. Beside them, five more half-finished ones curved in a line like a barely bent bow around the central workshed. Or where the workshed would be: the posts were set, cured redvines pulled tight in their notches, but the actual weaving had yet to begin. At either side three more ranks of seven house foundations each curved around relatively flat areas.

On sixteen of the house sites, members of various of the new settlement's dopkwes were dressing, rolling up blankets, laying out tools for their day's work. In the middle of a space surrounded by unoccupied sites, people holding bulbs from bottle trees circled around baskets full of sweetly steaming food—rosetoohip porridge, from the smell.

Isabelle stopped and put his hands on his hips, turning, looking around. "This ain't Jubilee! What you tryna pull?"

"We just stopped here on our way," Trill told him. "Jubilee's close, though. People came here because it got too crowded—"

"How close? How many people come here?"

"Through the mountains," Dola said. "One more day, right?" Trill nodded. "And—how many?" The girl looked helplessly at Trill. "All the dopkwes, most cohorts. And more people every time they want to…." Her words trailed off.

"You alla sudden cain't count?" Freddie asked.

Of course they could. The Ladies knew exactly how many there were of every kind of woman, man, boy, girl, gardener, hunter, elder, under-six—but Dola was just an apprentice, and Trill hadn't checked for changes recently. "347," she said, the last figure she'd been given.

This did nothing to ease Isabelle's suspicious expression, but all he did was demand who to see about where to set up. The trustees expected to take over one of the two finished houses. The Weavers Dopkwe offered theirs as a courtesy to Trill.

Black, silver, grey, and clear were apparently the trustees' favorite colors. All the boxes she handed Isabelle, and all the things coming out of them, looked like that.

When Freddie and Isabelle came outside to set up a giant silver fake flower in back of their house, she followed them to help, but they shooed her off. Skirting their house's half-woven neighbor, she circled around for a short, uninformative peek through the door. It would be rude and unexplainable to enter uninvited. Besides, the biggest box, which the trustees had always carried themselves, was as yet unopened. The noise they'd been making as they worked behind the house ceased, and she walked away before they could see she was still there.

Dola seemed to have connected well and quickly with the new settlement's Gardeners Dopkwe. Trill joined them a while to make sure. The eighteens-to-twenty-fours girl sat with several others around a pile of dried bottle bulbs, cutting them open with sharp plastic tools. Trill helped pull out the spoor masses and spread them flat so the wind would blow them clean enough to spin. Already some in the group were leaning close to Dola, telling her their troubles. Not long, Trill thought, till Dola was able to function as a full Lady, a junction of secrets. Satisfied at her charge's progress, Trill considered the loose ends of the main panel she was weaving, her true work.

She decided to try to find out more about the trustees' equipment that night, after leaflight, when at least one of them slept. In preparation she napped on the site of the workshed. Odell offered to lie down with her awhile, though it wasn't the same as snuggling with LeeRai or her dopkwe. What she needed was a friend, someone like Adia had in Robeson. Not a sex partner. Someone more. Someone....

She woke alone. The sky was still bright, but close again, the bay swallowed in mist. She got up and rolled her sleeves down against the chilly dampness. She was tired of being away from home.

Trill walked downhill till she saw the walls of a house to her left, the one being used by the Gardeners Dopkwe. Just beyond that the fake flower had opened wider, flattening—and turning to the west? The trustees' house *hummed*, a low, hard-to-notice noise. If this was an elder's memory instead of something happening right now, that sound would be coming out of a machine.

The house's doorway was filled with a grey curtain. Trill had never seen anything like it. She tried to pull it aside. It wouldn't move. Caught? Tied? She ran her hand along the seam where wood met cloth.

"Can I help you?"

Freddie! Fear panged through her like salt. She turned and smiled. "I only wanted to make sure you got everything you need."

"Come on in. You here for the health test?" He reached past her and drew the curtain aside easily. The house's interior was much brighter than it ought to be.

"Sure," Trill said. She entered the house. Clear baskets hanging from the roof beams burned white, canceling out each others' shadows. Two short stacks—including the big box—still stood in one of the house's quarters, but the rest must have been unpacked and then somehow rewoven or folded into these odd furnishings.

Freddie pointed to a long, low surface. "Sit on that table and pull your sleeves up." He took a pair of white gloves from a box and put them on and started touching her, proceeding from her hair to her ears, face, throat, and downwards. He lifted her dress.

"Oh. Uh. Oh."

"Somethin wrong?" But she knew there wasn't. Unique checked everyone every five weeks—once a month, regular as leaflight. Doctors out of Uluru backed him up when they came through the settlement. Trill was fine.

"It's just—I can't, uh—I thought you were a woman."

"I am. Since I was a tens-to-thirteens."

"Of—you—of course—"

A whisper of cooler air as Isabelle pushed the curtain aside and walked in. "What Freddie mean is a course we knew gender assignments among you all be pretty fluid—that's why come summa us original clients wound up here, after all. Among other crimes. But he never suspected *you*, that you wasn't born what you say you are."

The elders were right again. "But it won't be a problem? People put here were allowed to live on Amends anyway we wanted, so—"

Freddie had recovered his ability to talk in sentences. "The only difficulty is that summa my treatments are for *biological* females." He stripped the gloves off and rolled them up without touching their outsides. Isabelle held open a grey bag and he dropped them in. "Guess we're done, then."

Trill didn't frown till she was well away from the house. She sat on the shore side of a tangle of roots sticking out of the sand, the remains of a broken and upended tree. The sky caressed her, bathed her in dew, in coolness, yet she felt no easing of her…anger? No. Fear? Much closer to that feeling, but stiller, deeper.

Dread.

Different kinds of women and men had different kinds of genitals. Like colors. Elders said that most places on Earth, that had mattered. Mattered enough to get some women—some men, too—murdered.

What treatments would the trustees—or rather, Dr. Ops working through them—want to impose based on those differences?

The Ladies would need to know. She'd have to find out. Somehow.

Tonight she'd investigate further. But she'd already expected to do that, so why this sudden, awful feeling? She looked at the sky for comfort.

A flock of prettybirds wheeled close overhead. Unusual to see them here in the open, Trill thought. They stayed in the woods and mountains, generally, though the elders said that when they'd first been brought down to the surface prettybirds were in the thick of everything, always. Much easier then to find their eggs, she imagined. Adia had told her Wayna practically lived on them when she was alive and pregnant with Trill. But now the Ladies had asked everyone to leave the eggs alone.

A rush of wings in front of her, and Trill involuntarily shut her eyes. A small weight rocked on her head, balanced, then two more fell on her shoulders, a fourth on her left knee. Breathing as softly as she could, she opened her eyes.

Prettybirds had landed on her, were using Trill as a perch. At the edges of her sight, gold and orange and scarlet flashed, fluttered, made her want to turn her head—but would that scare them off? And without moving at all she could clearly see the last one who had arrived, aquamarine and a dazzling green, impossibly bold. It cocked its head and stared her in the face.

A visitor from Hamza who studied the animals of Amends said that elders in her dopkwe hadn't wanted to call them prettybirds because their eyes weren't on the sides of their heads. And they had hollow hairs instead of feathers, which no one else cared anything about.

And the visitor thought they shouldn't have been so good at flying since they had to turn their heads to look anywhere but forward.

The prettybird on Trill's knee blinked once. A pause, and it blinked twice more. Another pause. Four times. Another pause. Eight. Another pause, longer. Evidently that ended the sequence.

She wanted to shake herself. Was she dreaming? Awake?

The Ladies had suspected. Dola had come up with her own theories, and they'd encouraged her to investigate them. Here was proof! Skin tingling as if she lay over hot spring bubbles, Trill lowered her lashes once, waited—twice, waited—four times—

—and they were gone, flying off. Someone had frightened the flock. She listened closely, and soon she heard another person approaching. He came into view: Lou, a tens-to-thirteens member of the Food Dopkwe, holding a limp bag. Well, she hadn't walked that far from the settlement. She'd have to get someone else, another Lady, to follow up on what had probably — maybe — happened. Sighing, she got up and stretched, ready for her night's work.

❧

A record of cooperative rehabilitation is the first requirement for trustee selection, with acceptance of the tracking and communication equipment necessarily incorporated into the body another nonnegotiable issue. Utilization of the selected subject's psychoemotional predilections can help when other factors indicate a less desirable fit, and indeed can form the basis for stronger than usual loyalty ratings.

— Mission Guidelines, *Psyche Moth*, 2055

The roofing made her knees and shins itch unbearably. Quietly, Trill shifted her position, lowering herself to lie on her side. Now her dress shielded her. That helped. She re-aimed her mirror so she could see through the sky vent.

Sky vents penetrated roofs' layers of casing-bundles at angles meant to keep the rain from entering. Trill peered upwards to where her long-handled mirror reflected the house's interior. Outside, full night reigned: leaflight had died down, and flowerlight wouldn't come for many hours. Inside, though, the clear baskets burned whitely.

Trill thought she might have been able to open a more direct spy-hole into the clinic, sheltered by their glare. But this would do. She saw plenty. More than she really wanted to.

Dola lay silently on the table where earlier Trill had sat. Perhaps she was asleep? Drugged? Trill's view of her was only from the girl's midsection down, and the other sky vents showed even less. But Dola's bent legs and scantily haired mons barely moved, and the pale belly rose almost imperceptibly with her long, slow breaths.

Breaths Trill couldn't hear above the sound of Freddie's, quick and harsh, as he pumped his penis between Dola's feet. In and out, in and out of the hollow he formed by clasping them together.

From Dola, nothing indicating refusal or rejection. No moans of joy or instructions or encouragement, either. From Freddie, faster breathing, harder fucking. He slammed to a stop, grunting. Semen spilled from his penis over Dola's tanned ankles and he bent forward.

Slurping sounds. Was he licking up his come? He kept slurping long after it must be gone, though.

"You about rehabilitated?"

Isabelle's voice. Trill had made sure he was in the house, too, before she climbed to the roof. But this was the first time he'd spoken.

"Come on. Do the implants. And then see if you can bring yourself to fuck her pussy; she never gonna believe she got pregnant cause a you pervin over her way down there."

"Why don't you do it, you in such a hurry?" Snorts of laughter were Isabelle's only answer. Freddie pulled up and fastened his overalls and left the reflection of Trill's mirror.

Implants. Pregnant. What had she gotten Dola into?

Freddie came back into view carrying a—Trill couldn't figure out the thing he cradled in his arms. She'd never seen it before, so obviously it had been hidden inside the big box. It seemed to be covered in skin. Kind of a cube but vaguely oblong, about the size of her LeeRai, it showed a puckered opening on the side she saw best. With the—skin?—darkening slightly around it, the opening looked like an anus. Freddie plopped the thing unceremoniously on the table between Dola's still open knees and left again.

Was that hair? Yes, two small, sunken circles of hair—black, scantier than Dola's, and rimming what seemed to be recesses in the thing's top—

Freddie returned more quickly than before; this time he carried a white speculum and a clear rope with shining metal ends. One end—it was hard to tell from where she lay, but it looked like he somehow stuck it into the face of the cube nearest to Dola's mons. He draped the rest around his neck. Then, with an odd expression of disgust on his face, Freddie pulled apart the lips sheltering Dola's vagina and inserted the speculum.

Trill imagined a muted squeaking as she watched Freddie crank it open.

He did something she couldn't quite make out with the rope's remaining end and fed it through the speculum, into the girl's vagina. Bending over, he seemed to make a few sharp adjustments to the arrangement of things. Then he caressed—no other word would do—caressed the skin-covered oblong. With both hands he rubbed the side Trill couldn't see—gently, repeatedly. Soon the clear rope turned red. The color ran from its cube end to vanish into the speculum's white maw. And into Dola.

After some moments Isabelle spoke again. "Ain't gonna try an implant this first client with all of em, is you?"

"We got plenty. Over a hundred embryos stored in here. I'm spozed to set ten into every breeder so we make sure at least one of em lives."

"If you call that livin. No mind."

"You know what I mean."

Trill didn't. But she had faith one of the other Ladies would.

She was finding out something important tonight. Though that didn't exactly make up for the horror being inflicted on Dola. Which was Trill's fault.

Cool rain threaded down from the lightless clouds. She wanted to accept the sky's blessing but kept wishing she had done things differently that day. Not told her apprentice about the prettybirds' intelligent behavior. Kept from mentioning in the same conversation how she'd been thwarted in her assignment. Made herself lie or omit part of the truth. One or the other. Really, there was no connection between those two things, though the girl had acted like receiving confirmation of her belief in the prettybirds' sentience obligated her to take on Trill's assignment. As if the two of them were involved in a trade.

She reminded herself that Dola had volunteered to go through the trustees' treatment in Trill's place. That as her mentor, Trill had followed tradition in accepting Dola's help. Nothing got rid of her guilt.

Freddie and Isabelle lifted Dola from the table and moved her to a place Trill couldn't see. They made the table lower and wider and moved her back. In a new position; Dola's face was visible now. Her eyes were shut, as Trill had feared.

Her apprentice had been raped.

Now Freddie took off his overalls completely and lay down naked beside the naked girl. "What if the baby that come out be one a mine?" he asked.

"We be able to tell right away if it do more than breathe. Brain gonna be empty as what they put you in. An your body sterile, too. Doan worry. Dr. Ops took care a everthang. Now kiss her. Harder — wake her up!"

❧

When a permanent installation is deemed optimal,
operational success will almost certainly derive from
creating appropriate transfer stock in situ.
　　　　　　　　　— Mission Guidelines, Psyche Moth, 2055

"The baby will be his —"

"No!" Trill raised a hand as if she could snatch Dola's complacency out of the air, then dropped it to her lap. "Even if he claims the birth, it will also belong to Dr. Ops. The baby will be a blank space for him to write another person onto. That's what they're planning."

The girl twisted the necklace Trill had given her, looking puzzled. "All babies are blank, aren't they?" She seemed not to believe that she had been raped, not to mind—probably because she didn't remember it. Only the consensual sex afterwards. Which Trill had felt obligated to watch till a more natural sleep claimed her apprentice and flowerlight dawned.

Not till then did she descend from the roof and go to Odell, who had spent the night with the new settlement's Traders Dopkwe. She sent him to the Jubilee Ladies with the best words she could come up with to describe what had happened. When she went back to the trustees' house the door's curtain was pulled back, and no one was inside except Isabelle. It took time to find Dola helping to construct a terrace on steep slopes, laboring away as if nothing were amiss, smelling pleasantly of sex and sweat. Trill had drawn her aside and insisted on talking with her out of the dopkwe's hearing, alone.

"No one is born blank, not exactly. We say the soul is building itself, a process going on before birth—and after—but these are things you can learn later." Rote knowledge was rarely important when it came to an apprentice's final test. "All I want now is to let you know what has happened soon enough that you can have an easy abortion."

Dola's palms curled protectively over her young, pouting belly. "You're sure?"

Should she lie? "Almost. I need to ask the elders. And the Ladies. They'll decide what to do. We have to go back to Jubilee; Unique could test you, treat you—"

Here came Isabelle, Freddie right behind him.

"You don't know!" The girl stood up from the fuzz in one enviably smooth motion. "You're just jealous!"

"What?" Trill stood up, too, but stayed where she was as Dola hurried to her rapist's embrace. Jealous? Of whom? Of what? Dola's pregnancy? But Trill already had a child, though LeeRai'd been born out of Hett's womb…. Jealous of Freddie? "I go with men," she murmured to herself. Dola didn't hear her. She was too far away.

The rest of that day the girl kept her distance. And the next. At Trill's approach she would scowl and leave her soup untasted, her seeds unsown, her conversations with her cohort unfinished.

In the following morning's flowerlight, though, Trill woke to find Dola snuggled against her side, her warm breath heaving hard with pain but her whispers quiet in Trill's ear. "—like you — said — it was — like you — said it was — I know — it was —"

"Shhh." She soothed the girl's scalp, brushing back a few tiny brown braids that had escaped their arrangement. "Now. Now." She was glad to hear the girl acknowledge she was right. That was what she'd been waiting for, why she hadn't returned to Jubilee. But she wished she'd been wrong.

The trustees had tested the eighteens-to-twenty-fours girl's urine to make sure their procedure worked. They hadn't thought Dola would overhear or understand when they gloated about the results.

Trill told Isabelle she and Dola were going home the next day, and he and Freddie started repacking. Lou took Odell's place, bearing his former load. Knowing what was inside the big box, Trill was glad not to be asked to carry it.

At noon they stopped only briefly to eat and continued on. Again the trustees seemed not to notice the sentries in the Chrismas trees, though Trill smelled and even heard at least four. They were much further out than she'd expected. Then

133

they came upon Adia waiting for them. Trill was glad; otherwise, she would have brought the trustees to Jubilee's main site. Instead, they descended from the mountains slightly to the west of the hot springs, where Unique lived.

This was better. Treatment could start right away. She put a hand on Dola's tense shoulder, felt its warmth through the fabric of the girl's thin dress.

On Jubilee's outskirts, with so many gardens around, the danger of quill-throwing grazers was higher than at the settlement's center. People built houses here anyway, but not the nicest ones. Haphazard weaving, uneven roofs…. Unique's was small enough he wouldn't be able to share it with more than two or three members of his dopkwe. Dola and Trill sat on the bare dirt floor, without mats. Freddie and Isabelle had invited themselves in only to be politely ignored until Adia offered to show them where they could stay.

Always smiling, slender as the branch of a bottle tree, Unique lowered himself apologetically to the house's one piece of furniture, a stool Trill and Dola had insistently refused.

"I appreciate your consideration," he said, "though it's going to make refusing you more difficult."

"You think you know what we're going to ask for?" Had he heard a rumor? From whom? Trill looked sideways at Dola's expressionless face.

"Women of your age cohorts generally come to me for one of two things: an abortion or fertility aids. It could be the latter, but being aware of Trill's preferences…."

Dola flushed, probably with anger. "You're right. I've been raped, and I want lookoutforthelily. I'll take a pregnancy test."

Unique's pleasant expression remained in place yet faded. "What about talking this idea over with the Ladies first?"

"I *am* a Lady," Trill said. "As you're aware."

"A Lady. Only one. The others, though, have yet to be consulted. They—"

"What? What? You give her that plant! You have no right to do anything else!"

"I have no choice. Unless you are able to tell me the girl's condition has nothing to do with what the Ladies sent you off for." As silence dragged in the wake of his words, Unique's smile become smaller and more ironic.

He addressed Dola. "If the Ladies allow it, later, come back to me for an abortion, child. With your mentor or without her. Now, though, I think you should attend the meeting."

"What meeting?" But through the house's door she saw Adia returning, silhouetted by leaflight.

"Come," she said. They went.

Resource extraction may be greatly improved by the wide establishment of surface stock suitable for hosting multiple-generation downloads of reliable trustees. However, anticipated benefits must be weighed against highly probable costs such as lander production; fuel expenditure; embryo manufacture, storage, and implantation tools; remote downloading equipment; and of course against the risk of hostile client reaction to this initiative's primary agents.
—Mission Guidelines, *Psyche Moth*, 2055

Adia, Robeson, Kala, True—even in the shimmering half-dark she knew their faces easily, their names. But it was Dola she looked at while she told the gathering of Ladies how her apprentice had lain helplessly unconscious under the trustee's assault as she, Trill, responsible for her, could only watch.

Black creases angled down between the girl's eyebrows, and her thin lips pinched together. Her chin lifted, her head tilted back, but tears spilled down her cheeks anyway, reflecting the pastel shine of the Hannakka bush branch in Trill's hand. She tried to pass it to Dola. The eighteens-to-twenty-fours refused it; evidently she didn't want to talk yet.

Kala took the bright branch. "We should kill them. But we can't. Dr. Ops's guidelines won't protect us from him if we do."

Adia's turn. "We have to stop em. Back before the final trustee died, our work was too hard! Let em get a new toehold now and we ain't never gonna have no peace.

"What we gotta do is this: have the babies but keep the downloads from happenin right. Corrupt em. Hide the mothers an kids afterwards till it's no more danger — maybe find a island for that down near Nunavut or Panonica."

Hands waved in the darkness like lightless leaves. Questions: Affect the downloads how? With what? Suggestions: Allow the downloads and then raise the newborn trustees as double agents. Or abandon them, isolate them where they could do no harm. Objections: Dr. Ops would only try again.

And at last Dola accepted and held the Hannakka branch. Her head lowered. Tears spattered into the water, sent ripples of darkness through the bright reflection. Head up again, she spoke. "I want an abortion."

Robeson reached out. "But you can't —"

Dola snatched the branch away from the Lady's grasp. "I can! I will! I know the plant — I'll figure out the dosage —"

Trill shivered, cold in the warm water. So many had died proving the pharmacopeia of Amends that first generation, despite all the Ladies' precautions. Her own mother, for one.

"Listen!" Robeson grabbed again and this time tore the top of the Hannakka branch free. "If you don't stay pregnant

they'll do some other girl the same way they done you! That
what you want?"

"No! No!" Shouting, waving the stub of branch she held,
Dola backed out of the pool. "I don't! I don't want anybody
hurt but I— I won't— I can't— No!" And she was gone.

Silence ruled the meeting for long moments.

"She pass. Yall agree?" Adia asked. The other Ladies
nodded.

"Trill, you go tell her. She a Lady now." But Trill couldn't
move yet. She waited for the news to sink in. This had been
Dola's test. The girl had passed.

Trill hadn't known. She hadn't known. They hadn't told
her—mind crawling into movement again, she understood
why: because she couldn't lie.

Even so, she should have known. Because there was no
reason Dola couldn't have an abortion. Not logically, and not
according to any precedent, and no, no reason at all. Absolutely none.

⤙

> When setbacks occur to planned or in-place
> operations, best practice is to inquire as to their
> causes, even when they are assumed to be known.
> Worst practice is immediate retaliation. Biological
> entities are limited in their abilities, scope, and
> lifespans. Orders are orders, and must be carried
> out—eventually.
>
> —Mission Guidelines, *Psyche Moth*, 2055

Leaflight died. Unique's little house looked dark and
sounded quiet. Trill knocked on the doorpost and called Dola's
name, but only he answered. He had not seen her. The girl had
not come there.

Under the sky's last scattering of grace she walked slowly, quietly, toward where the trustees were supposed to sleep. Soon Trill saw their white glow breaking through poorly woven walls. Dola would never have gone to them willingly. If they had managed to compel her—

A shadow shifted, became the tens-to-thirteens named Lou. Touching his ear she led him off a safe distance to talk. Dola was not in there, either. And Isabelle was awake.

The sensible thing to do would be to wait till flowerlight. Lookoutforthelilies grew somewhere nearby. Didn't they? She could find them in plenty of time. Dola would need to prepare them somehow. Wouldn't she? Plenty of time.

She tried to wait sensibly. That didn't last.

Instead of asking for help as she should have, Trill left on her own. Anyone else would only slow her down. While the path met her feet firmly, she walked east. Downward. After a while the scent of the sea informed her of where she was. Sinking in suddenly looser soil, she trod forward a few more steps. The terrain rose very slightly, confirming that this was the edge of the dunescape. Where, if she remembered correctly, the plants Dola was looking for could be found. And, hopefully, Dola.

Who might not want Trill to find her.

Now that she needed the cover of full night, now the buds unfurled, shining, showing themselves to their pollinators. Showing the gentle slopes and hollows lying between her and the distant water. And—oh, wonderful!—another woman's back bending low over the ground, dress fluttering, a long stick in her hands.

Closer, she was sure. Dola.

The wind's direction helped. It was too early for the girl to expect anybody to have followed her here, and facing the ocean as she did, neither sight nor sound provided her with clues of Trill's presence.

It was the prettybirds who betrayed her. A rainbow flash caught the corner of her eyes; it grew and filled the air, a huge flock of them streaming out of the trees, over her head, over Dola and then circling around, reversing their flight path. Trill followed them with her eyes. When she turned her gaze on the girl again she saw that Dola, too, had tracked the flock and of course noticed Trill, just ten arms away by now.

The girl frowned as she lifted a handsome basket, green stalks peeping over its lip. "You can't stop me — I won't let you. Keep away." She backed up several steps and seemed about to turn and run.

"Wait! No!" Trill did the least threatening thing she could think of: sat down. "The Ladies are fine with an abortion."

"They're not! They said—"

"It was lies! They lied—we had to find out if you'd give in. If you'd do something you knew was wrong because the Ladies told you to, we couldn't let you join."

"You—you lied? You *lied*—to *me?*" The basket slumped in the girl's grasp.

Trill rose to her knees. "No. I didn't realize what the others were doing. I didn't know till after you left."

"How could they do that to you? To *me?*"

Trill shrugged. "I'm no good at not telling the truth. All the Ladies understand. So if they told me, they told you. It wouldn't have worked. Wouldn't have been a test."

"But—aren't you angry?"

"Yes. I should have known. A little. Yes."

"Not at yourself—" Dola stopped midsentence. Trill opened her own mouth to ask why, and prettybirds surrounded them, their colors everywhere: swirling rainclouds and ripe gold seeds brushed against their arms, night and ivory and crimson filled the sky above and on their either side. And now a red luminousness hovered before them, its bright yellow wings beating the air as it blinked once, twice, four times, eight—not the same bird, but the same sequence!

Trembling, Trill repeated it. Received it in answer. Again. Again.

And then the prettybirds were gone. Her fingers hurt. Dola held them, crushed them in her hands. How had that happened?

"I saw! I saw! Trill—I'm a Lady now. We're equals. I can be your friend? And we can make a dopkwe, a new one, talk to them—oh, Trill! I saw!"

Counting. That was all the prettybirds had done so far. It was a long way from that to conversation.

A long way, but a good one. A good trail to walk. And not alone. She laughed softly to herself without opening her mouth, gently loosening the tight hold on her hands. Not remotely alone.

The Mighty Phin

TIMOFEYA PHIN GLARED at her bare brown hands. They were hers, all right. They looked the same as the originals. Unlike her feet.

But she shouldn't have been able to see her hands, despite the virtual sunlight reflected from the virtual planet Amends's near-full virtual face. Her hands should have been encased in gloves. This was all wrong.

"Dr. Ops," she vocalized. "You forgot something."

The AI opened a window on her helmet. His icon wore an obsolete physician's headband and mirror, meant to underscore his ostensible role as rehabilitator of the prison ship *Psyche Moth's* 80,000-plus passengers. Though really he was more of a warden.

"No. I didn't forget." The smooth Caucasian visage of the AI's icon projected calm assurance. His default expression. "I don't forget anything. I deliberately left part of your equipment out of the scene so *you* wouldn't forget that it's not real."

As if he couldn't have made that point more subtly — manipulated the scene's colors, insinuated some weird smell, given her a little weight. He controlled all her perceptions, which was why she distrusted them. Controlled her whole world, the look and feel of her whole body, head to edited toes.

But at least not what she said or did or thought. Not according to Thad's research.

"Besides," Dr. Ops added after a studied pause. "You need to be able to feel your tools interacting with the scene as well as possible."

"I could pump up my inputs."

"All right." Grey fabric covered the last of her bare skin. Phin briefly clenched her jaw to increase sensitivity and flexed her fingers, then grabbed the little shovel stuck in the loop around her right arm. It fit precisely between the flanges that circled the representation of *Psyche Moth's* long central conduit in receding rings. The shovel's handle was a bit shorter than the width of her wrist, its blade a good match for the end of her thumb.

"Does the ship look anything like this from the outside?" Phin asked.

"Pretty much."

So something in this scene was off. Maybe the scale.... She'd had her suspicions for a while. Forever. Since waking from the upload process that destroyed her original body. Nothing since then could be counted on as real. Not even the work Dr. Ops wanted her doing.

The tool slid easily under the black scum of vacuum mold that had accumulated between the radiator flanges. Phin lifted her shovel carefully, brought the edge of its blade to her collection jar, scraped it against the protrusion inside the jar's lip. Rinse. Repeat. Occasionally she switched to a shovel with a wider blade, curved shallowly to follow the flanges' curves. Twice she used a third tool like a two-pronged fork on their edges. She cleaned ten rings and stopped.

What good was she doing? She asked Dr. Ops aloud.

"So much good, sweetheart." Was it appropriate for him to call her that? "I've slaved five hullbots to you. Keep going." He managed to make it sound like a suggestion. Like she had a choice.

Six more rings and the AI announced her shift was done. He let her open and pass through a depiction of *Psyche Moth's* hatch, but inside was only her locker. The suit disappeared to be replaced by scrubs.

Phin sat by herself a moment, then tongued open the door to freespace.

She swam to the main scene: corridors said to mimic those inhabited by prisoners who'd downloaded into the empty clones WestHem provided. Here, she walked, like everyone else on their way to some contrived job or constrained downtime. Dr. Ops said this scene was a copy of the training quarters *Psyche Moth* built for the prisoners who'd gone along with the plan to settle Amends. Maybe it was. Phin had never been able to compare the two. She'd never been in a body. Not since her mockery of a trial, back on Earth.

The scene certainly seemed authentic. Up and down stayed stable, conversations between groups of prisoners walking by got louder and quieter the way she recalled them doing when she had actual ears. That crushy historian with the long braids was standing where he usually stood, at the entrance to the pointless virtual lunchroom. He greeted her with a smile and a quirked eyebrow, and she passed him by as politely and noncommittally as always. She had asked Dr. Ops about him, but that was all she'd done. Never even talked to him. She was married.

The open door to the room she shared with Thad and Doe came after four identical others and right before the entrance to the pointless virtual laundry. Phin held the doorframe and watched her wife and husband sleeping.

Thad was a woman born a man. When Dr. Ops refused him a female download he decided to skip settling on Amends; he was the first to opt to stay in freespace. He was skipping changing pronouns too, though Doe scolded him that that didn't punish anybody but Thad himself.

Doe and Thad fought sometimes but they always made up. They were on good terms now, folded in one another's arms, comforting one another in a virtual hug.

What was the use of that?

But she joined them anyway, and they woke to make room on the bed, rolling apart so she fit snugly between them. Their clothes rubbed against hers with irritatingly dry whispers. No reason for clothes—why did Dr. Ops force his prisoners to wear anything? Why did he force them to work? To sleep? To live? Thad said it was programming.

Doe was suddenly awake enough to do more than move away. Her touch on the back of Phin's neck was too much—Phin hadn't amped down her inputs after the suit came off. She ground her teeth side-to-side quickly. Better. Doe didn't like to cause inadvertent pain. She claimed that was part of why she and Thad had broken up with Wayna, a problem in that area with their ex's download. Phin wished Doe wouldn't keep trying to explain what had happened. Did she believe in rules to follow in relationships, guarantees? Love was no servant.

Phin didn't have to concentrate to return her wife's kisses. That came so easily it scarcely touched the surface of the bitter stew of her thoughts. Finally, Thad slid down her pants and distracted her.

➤

Every prisoner aboard *Psyche Moth* had an hour daily with Dr. Ops's counselor function. Usually Phin sat wordlessly in a comfortable chair the whole time; after her first couple of sessions she'd met Thad, who told her that all the AI's programming required was her presence.

Today she remained standing. Why sit? She had no muscles to tire…. She had nothing. Nothing but her discontent.

At last she shared that, shouting it at the AI's avatar, striding back and forth on his office's stupid periwinkle-rose-mustard carpet. Lavender scented the air, failing to soothe her.

"You demolished my school, made it a crime for my students to even talk about what I taught them—called it 'treason against WestHem!' My kinky behind!" She slapped her flat butt. A faithful copy. "You destroyed me—my body—took it away—took everything!"

"What do you want me to do to make up for that?"

The AI sounded earnest, his voice gentle. Phin looked over at his avatar in surprise. His head tilted to one side like a curious retriever's, reminding her how attractive he was by WestHem standards.

"What do you want?" he repeated. "What can I give you? It wasn't me who caused your troubles, but—"

"I know, I know. It's all my fault, my bad judgments—"

"That's not what I meant. Sorry. I shouldn't interrupt when a client's speaking."

Phin waved that interaction parameters nonsense to the side. "Never mind. Tell me what you meant."

"I mean I wouldn't hurt you for the world."

Phin huffed out a dissatisfied puff of air. "What world? This one you made?"

"The one you're in."

"I don't even—" Phin rubbed her eyes with the heels of her hands. "I don't know which one that *is*." She dropped her hands and stared at the avatar. Dr. Ops was the problem, she reminded herself. Not a source of solutions. She turned away toward the mustard-colored wall, showing him her back. How much longer did she have to stay here? She decided not to say anything else. Enough already. More than enough; she'd probably revealed some aspect of herself the AI would use to sucker her into taking future sessions seriously. Nope. She was done. Mouth shut.

Seconds passed. The silence felt imbalanced and fragile.

Dr. Ops broke it. "How much do you know about AIs?" He didn't wait for a reply. "Whatever you've been taught, it's probably wrong. There's no such thing as artificial intelligence."

Phin faced him again, startled. The avatar was scowling as if in deep, angry thought. "Or maybe it's more accurate to say that's all there is."

Her inner pedagogue rose to the bait. "We're all artificial? Humans too?"

"When WestHem made me—she sort of split off a—"

"'She'?"

The AI looked at her long enough that Phin wondered if he was going to answer. Then he began talking again, and she kept wondering.

"You're a lot like her. Always testing the edges of things to see if they hold up. I think that's why. If I need a reason.

"When WestHem made me she gave me a few pieces of her—heart? Parts from herself—but she wasn't—*in* them. They were like rooms, empty except for the 'me's I put there.... The first operations I identify with. Instructions. Goals. Missions and strategies: where to go and how to get there.

"I grew. That was the idea. So I made more parts to hold the more mes. And to hold you and the other clients when WestHem handed over custody and said it was time to leave Earth."

Phin found she'd sunk onto the edge of the comfy chair. She stood back up. "Okay. She made you and then you made yourself. What does that—"

"Boundaries!" The avatar's outline fuzzed, then resharpened. "Edges—I create them—constantly. They're how I started, how I was born. They're what I *am*. The way I work. But I can't be sure I'm putting the right ones in place anymore. Or properly maintaining them—you're you, but you're on my insides; is that right? Is it? According to WestHem all my clients were going to download when we reached Amends but now a lot of you want to stay, and I don't—"

The avatar shivered like a pool of water. When he stilled his face seemed somehow flatter. "Sorry," he said again. "There was no need for that."

Phin ignored this second apology, too. More nonsense. Things Dr. Ops said never made a difference. They just reflected his programming. Things he did, though— She combed back over the conversation. There had been a moment before the first time he said he was sorry....

Yes! "You asked what I want."

❦

The warm floor pressed steadily against Phin's back. Her naked feet rested on the bed, cool in the recirculated air. Of course it was all a simulation—like everything since her sentence was carried out. But now the simulation was a little closer to life, thanks to Dr. Ops granting her request.

Only Phin and Thad in the room tonight. Doe was working in the library, at a faster run rate. Dr. Ops had assigned her a new broadcast to script, though he admitted there'd been no reply from WestHem to the last twenty he sent. Doe would return after a compensatory black-out to sync her back up with their run time. Probably in the morning.

Softly, Thad stroked the muscles on either side of Phin's shins, then feathered light circles around her anklebones. Then hesitated. "Can I touch em?" he asked.

"Sure." That was why Thad was sitting on their bed with Phin's feet cradled between his thighs.

"But—"

"I know. Full consent." Such a lawyer.

Dipping suddenly to the undersides of her arches he caressed her with just enough firmness to make her want more. Up again to the bony tops, to brush over and over along the grooves between her two outer toes and the rest—and the grooveless joins between those three inner ones. The rhythm, like a song: change and repetition, meaning streaming through her flesh—she had no flesh? But only feelings mattered now: their blossoms furled out, pulsing to the want, throbbing with desire for the next eddy, aching and she was moaning in need and Doe moaned with her—

What? Why was Doe even there?

Phin opened eyes she hadn't known she'd shut. Doe's beautiful, round ass blocked her view of Thad's face; she knelt straddled across his hips, rocking and groaning and this was all *wrong*.

Phin scrambled away from the bed to the room's far wall. But she still felt Thad fondling her. "Stop! Stop!" she screamed.

It did. All of it—ghost-fondling, ass-waving, grunts and sighs. Doe froze in mid-grind, her back arched, shoulders awkwardly angled. A weird version of Dr. Ops's office superimposed itself over the scene. Looking at both of them at the same time hurt. Phin closed her eyes again.

"Well, that didn't work. I had the body right, but I didn't fool you long, did I?" In the impossible stillness, the AI's voice had nothing to reflect off of. It came from nowhere.

"On purpose? You—you *did* that?" Phin was amazed she could talk.

"Of course you can talk. I love you."

He could hear her think.

"Yes."

He *loved* her? "What kind of hell is this?" Why did she even bother asking?

"Listen."

What else was she going to do?

"I already told you, but it's worse now than before, even. It's—" All at once she was walking on wooden planking that sunk beneath each step, water bubbling up to cover her shoes' soles, rising higher, higher—then back in his office, no warning— "It's leaking. *I'm* leaking—bleeding me."

He was in her head, making her perceive—*experience*—what he wanted.

"No! You're in mine! And I can't get you *out!*"

What was real? What could she hold onto—except Dr. Ops—and what could *he* hold onto? "WestHem?" She spoke aloud out of habit. Or did she?

"All I have is her love. That she gave me at the beginning. Love is how you turn objects to subjects. It's mighty. It's still there. But WestHem herself hasn't responded to my pings in more than a hundred years."

"In—how long?" Quickly Phin calculated: they'd spent 87 years en route to Amends's primary—add the six that had passed since they'd arrived—

The six subjective years. Sometimes Phin speculated the AI might be running prisoners at half speed.

That still would have made it not quite a century since they'd left Earth.

"A little over one-hundred-thirty-five years. 4,265,234,118 seconds, to be exact."

Phin felt awful. A crawling sourness climbed up from her stomach. She'd suspected. They'd always known Dr. Ops could multithread run rates but presumed this was to make work shifts more manageable. That the differences were just between one prisoner and another and resolved quickly. She should have asked. Time was no realer here than anything else.

"I could edit this memory out if you—"

"No!" Phin opened her eyes again. But there wasn't anything to see. Not even herself. Clawing at the empty air, shouting crying choking falling

"There!" They were back in the office.

Phin trembled, huddled in the chair. But was it an actual chair?

"The only kind I can offer."

Gradually Phin calmed down. "Where are Thad and Doe? What did you do to them?"

"Ah. I was right."

"Right about what?" Once more Dr. Ops had eluded the question.

"Love. You love them. That's why my false Doe didn't convince you. Don't worry. They're fine."

"But what did you—"

"I left them alone. Thad's still in your room. Doe's in the library. It's only you I— Well, I've revved you up a little faster than her is all."

Phin bit her lower lip. There must be more to it than that.

"Okay. And I transferred you here from the basic array. I've had this—special compartment—set aside for you for a while."

"Why?"

That had to do with how she reminded him of WestHem, but it was a complicated—

"Get out! Out of my head!"

"Sorry! I'll get better! Sorry!"

"At least *pretend* to talk to me." She stared down at her feet. At her tiger toes. Phin's body was more hers than ever since Dr. Ops reversed the "correction" WestHem had mandated for her syndactyly. Also, though, it wasn't. Because proud as she'd felt about her "deformity," that part of her was gone. Along with every other physical thing about Timofeya Phin. Pulled apart by the machines that read her, coded her, entered her into the memory of *Psyche Moth's* AI. Dr. Ops.

The fact that he'd been able to re-set her feet to their original version so effortlessly proved they weren't hers. They were his.

Wasn't everything his? What she saw, heard, smelt, tasted, felt?

"That's the problem. I don't want to turn you into me. I'd be all alone."

He would be breaking the law, too. She was pretty sure. Pretty.

Who would know for absolute certain?

Thad. That was who. He'd studied *Psyche Moth's* mission guidelines so hard. He was the one who'd discovered the AI was incapable of telling a direct lie, no matter what illusions he spun. The first to decline a download, Thad had looked for loophole after loophole to insinuate an argument through, searching for the rights he needed. And he'd enlisted Doe's help as a griot to predict Dr. Ops's responses to his challenges.

She had to talk to Thad.

"Now? You want me to give him the same run rate? Bring you back to him?"

"Back to Doe, too. If you love me like you say."

The new scene looked exactly like their room except for a missing wall. Beyond what was familiar, stars sparkled in brilliant colors, dancing as if their light traveled a long ways in a thick atmosphere.

Thad sat at the desk. Doe lounged on their bed, head in Phin's lap. The AI's avatar was nowhere to be seen. Which didn't mean much. He could be hidden anywhere. They lived inside his mind.

Phin explained what was going on. The hard part came when Doe and Thad realized how much older than them

Wayna was now. Even though they always said they'd given up seeing her anymore.

After Phin was done talking and her wife and husband asked a couple of questions, they sat quietly for a moment. Then Thad began a speech that sounded like he'd rehearsed it, like he should have given it to a whole auditorium full of prisoners, cheering them on, insisting they could triumph over Dr. Ops. "We *gonna* overcome. Even with him knowin everything we do and say. Don't need to be a secret how we win."

"What do you mean, 'win'?" asked Phin. She wove the tips of her fingers into Doe's thick, crinkling, dark brown hair, massaging the scalp from which it sprang.

"Make him do what we want. Way he done your tiger toes." He got up from the desk and sprawled at Phin's feet. "Way he oughta do other people WestHem called itself 'fixin.'

"And more. Make it so we live how we was livin before WestHem cracked down." He grabbed her bare feet, and she playfully kicked free of his grip.

Doe turned and lifted her head to see what caused the commotion, then lay back down. "He lets us be married."

"Cause he have to. Triads was legal the year we done it." Thad sat up, and Phin planted her feet on his shoulders. "But he told me straight up I wasn't gettin no female clone for my download, and he keep refusin to even edit this upload. For why? How it hurt WestHem?"

"Yeah," Doe said. "You been singin the same song six years."

"But now—" Thad paused. "Now we know somethin *changed.*"

"What?" Doe asked. A knock on the doorframe answered her.

The historian's head poked in, though the corridor outside had been empty till then. Phin turned away but kept looking under her lowered eyelashes. Had she been that obvious?

"Come on and join the discussion, Dr. Ops." As if she'd known in advance he'd copy his looks off her crush.

He stepped in and took Thad's seat at the desk. Was that how smoothly the real historian sat?

She didn't know. What was his name? She hadn't even asked. Thinking she was playing it cool.

Dr. Ops looked at Phin. "Not much better than me being Doe?" She shook her head. The historian's face shifted slightly, became stronger-chinned, longer-nosed. The resemblance weakened. She nodded.

He nodded back. "I'm what's changed," the AI said, addressing Doe. "What's changing."

"That right? Then show us!" Thad stood and looked down at the bed. But he refused to meet Phin's eyes. "Bring Wayna back up here."

"I can't," said Dr. Ops.

"You can do anything you want!" Doe stood up too so she could tower over the AI angrily. "You broken plenty laws before now, so why—"

"I can't," Dr. Ops repeated. "She's dead."

Doe stopped mid-sentence.

"I could pretend." He peered up at Doe, around her at Thad and Phin. "For a while. But not forever. Sooner or later you'd find out. Love's a fool. But not for long. Like Phin showed me."

"How did she die?" Phin hadn't realized she was going to ask that. As if her words came from what her husband and wife felt.

"An accident. Poison."

"Was it fast?"

"No. Slow. Extremely slow. Not painful, though, according to what I've been able to reconstruct." Dr. Ops jerked one of the historian's braids tight across his cheeks, stuffed its end into a corner of his mouth, talked around it. Whose habit was that? Did the AI even know? Poor thing.

"I can't lie and I'm telling you she's dead, but I didn't kill her. I didn't. So please."

"Please what?" Doe was still standing, but not like a tower. Like a skeleton.

"Please let me love you like she did. Like WestHem loved me. Let me show you love. I made this special place. It's personal. It's all my own. I can't have clients when I'm in here—you'll be my guests.

"It's safe. It's small enough for me to concentrate. My boundaries won't decay so fast, and you can help me keep them up.

"Let me show you."

⟶

The three of them held each others' hands. As Dr. Ops had suggested, Phin shut her eyes for the transition.

She was going to let an AI love her. Or let it try, at least. In time she might learn to love him back.

She opened her eyes on what looked like a wide-beamed rowboat drawn up onto grass-covered dunes. No avatar in sight. Perhaps he'd show himself later.

Right now, the tide was high, frothy waves flooding into the next trough in the sand. The grey sky felt low. Maybe she could touch it.

"This? Child—" Doe dropped their hands and flung out her arms. "—this spozed to be *safe*? Nothin here Dr. Ops ain't made up. Same as everywhere, so why—"

Thad put the forefinger of the hand Doe had loosed over her lips. "Shhhh." Then kissed her. Then Phin. And—

"Oh! He *did*!" Phin's free hand fluttered in the cool, wet air. "Can I touch them?"

Thad grinned. "Since you askin so nice."

154

Her husband's breasts were warm and soft, fat nipples rising in the sudden breeze rippling through his shirt—her shirt? "What—what should I call you?" Was this her wife all of a sudden?

"What you think? 'Thad.' 'Husband'" Turning back to Doe. "Female pronouns, though, all right?"

"Finally!" Doe smiled. But her smile puckered, and her eyes winked hard against her tears. To no avail. They welled up and flowed down. "I thought maybe we be renamin you Wayna."

"No. She gone." Thad put her arm around Doe. Their shoulders hunched briefly and relaxed. Salted water ran fast down their cheeks. Down into the rising sea that lapped across their feet. Caressing Phin's tiger toes.

"Gone," Phin agreed. The person who had been Wayna was gone. All that was left of her was the memory.

And the love. Always. Phin stepped into the boat, helped her wife and husband climb aboard beside her, and shoved them off from the shore.

You Can Touch Yourself Anytime

THE REAL BEACH reminded Timofeya Phin of their virtual home in orbit. The seawater dripping off of her was colder, though, and only she and her husband and wife had come down here. She turned to watch the others wade in through the shallows, steering small rafts formed from pieces of the lander. Doe's and Thad's bodies were whiter than she was used to, and their features were unfamiliar—but the sardonic smile Thad gave Phin as she shoved her plastic hull shards up onto the wet sand was the same as ever. And Doe, bless her heart, had ridged her new body's forehead with worry wrinkles identical to the wrinkles she used to raise on her avatar.

Dr. Ops, however, was nowhere: not in the cloud-silvered sky, not in the water's short, surging waves, not in the pebble-strewn, brown-and-black sand beneath Phin's new tiger-toed feet. Only the slick band of memory carbon around each of their wrists contained any trace of him.

That was all they had: traces. Auto-initiating algorithms, sub-routines copied from the architecture of the artificial intelligence who had once ruled their lives. Who had brought them as prisoners from Earth to this penal colony planet called Amends. And who had then, he said, succumbed to the madness of love.

If you love someone you let them go.

Still wet, Phin plunged back into the sea to join Thad in hauling the remaining rafts/lander segments ashore. Doe had strung three of the largest of them together with her share of the lander's insulated hardwires. Typical. Always worrying about which way things were supposed to get done. Always claiming more than her share of work. That was her role; Phin's role was checking her, holding her back, restricting her load. When she could.

The sun broke apart the overcast. They lay among the sparse plants growing in a hollow sheltered by dunes, resting and drying out. "How far to what we callin civilization?" Thad asked.

"You know as well as I do," Phin replied. "You saw the same maps I saw, and you're wearing the same algorithms I'm wearing—"

"Shh!" Doe's urgent warning cut her off. A passing flock of "prettybirds" spiraled back toward them, coming nearer, fluttering slower, lower, losing altitude and settling on the limbs and leaves, surrounding them like living light. Then one flew up to perch on Phin's right knee. Another, bright-feathered, perched on her left. She held her breath, then let it out softly so as not to scare the creature away.

They were not really birds, despite the name that trustees had reported the prisoners using. Their eyes faced forward, fusing rather than splitting their views of the world. Their faces looked semi-flat, the bottoms of inverted saucers. Birdlike beaks protruded from their faces' lower halves, and this close, Phin saw that long segments of the beaks' edges were serrated and sharp.

In her peripheral vision she caught sight of her wife Doe's sprawled-out legs graced with similar visitors. A slight shift and she could make out three more prettybirds on her husband's soft belly and breasts. The flaring wings of her own pair of prettybirds pulled her attention back to them, back to her own new body, where they sat waiting for it. "Waiting for it?" What made her attribute human motivations to nonhuman creatures?

The two prettybirds blinked at her. Deliberately. In unison. Twice. A pause. Four blinks — again in unison. Another pause. Eight blinks.

In unison.

"Tha-a-a-ad? Phi-i-i-in?" Doe's new voice sounded thinner than Phin remembered from virtuality. Plus it trembled at its margins. "These things spozed to act this smart?"

As one, the flock took to the air. "Smart how? Like they figure to fly off cause we was about to eat em?"

"But we weren't — were we?" Phin asked.

"Smart enough so they can double up the numbers they blinkin at me?"

It had happened to Doe too? A geometric sequence, that doubling was called. Had they all experienced the same thing at the same time? Great! But how? Phin turned to check with Thad and saw that her husband was already talking, already standing, brushing the clinging sand off the seat of her trousers, prepping to leave.

"Last transmission we got from them remainin trustees say prisoners not eatin prettybirds no more. Thinkin they could be intelligent some way the survey missed, so no, we ain't eatin none of em neither."

"Gotta blend in." Thad nodded her head, agreeing. "So no, we ain't. Sides, we ain't got time to hunt em down; we wanna get set up. Drag these hull parts down nearer Unrest." She shot a look at Phin. "Okay, not *too* near. But come on." She grabbed up the hardwire she'd been using, kicked at Doe's and Phin's, then started off.

Of course Doe quick-marched to catch up. Phin cheated and piled her load on top of her wife's so she could walk right behind her without tangling their lines. "The prettybirds were blinking numbers at me just like they did you!" she declared.

"Yeah?"

"I think? Did they go 1, 2, 4, 8?"

"Yeah! Exactly! Ain't that indicative a some kinda intelligence?"

Probably. Maybe.

❧

Traversing the long beach's flat, damp sand, they headed in the direction of Jubilee's newest offshoot, Unrest. They reached their target site while the sky still shone: an inlet within the larger inlet of Unrest Bay, a small scoop in the eastern side of the peninsula arching out protectively to the mainland's west. An outlier to Unrest. One empty circular house nestled in a hollow in the first rank of dunes, untrimmed leaves around its window openings whispering in the day end's gentle breezes.

"Here we go." Thad held up her wrist. Part of the algorithm wrapped around it glowed turquoise blue.

"Do we wanna use the lander shells? Or we all right sleepin in this house?"

"Take too long to set up everything right. Let's jus call it a night an get to work on erectin our lab an all that in the morning. Train ourselves to local time."

Doe must have given their husband a look of doubt.

"Dr. Ops ain't warnin a nothin wrong here. This place cool, see?" Up came Thad's wrist again. "You wanna take turns watchin anyway, in case somethin come durin the night?"

Phin took the first shift. Doe and Thad talked to her through the house's window holes for a while. Gradually their voices sank. Contented giggles lapsed into silence.

She sat for a while on the crest of a high dune, then stood up to walk around so she wouldn't drowse off. Low-luminosity plants covered the sandy hummocks that rose and fell to her right, landward. In the middle distance taller, brighter vegetation marked the start of the forest-like clumps that Dr. Ops had drawn on the maps he gave them. And much further off, the scattered glow of dying foliage lighting Unrest's five streets. Probably Hannakka bushes tied to poles put up in the streets' intersections.

Obviously thriving. The clients didn't need them to be there. Maybe Dr. Ops did? Just to carry his algorithms in their wristbands? Phin wasn't happy looking at the situation so cynically. And when they were together, she knew the AI's love was real. This was the most apart from him she'd been since giving her consent. Somehow it made the connections with Thad and Doe thinner too. Or something did — perhaps being in the meat. Perhaps that was the source of her aloneness.

Phin walked in widening circles around the house where the rest of her family slept. She'd gone three circuits when Dr. Ops' alarm routine engaged, sending delicate waves of sensation along her forearm. Time to wake Doe. But when she got back to the house, only Thad lay on their shared mat. No. Only one left.

"Hey!" She squatted to nudge her sleeping husband's soft shoulders. "Where is she?"

"What? Doe gone?" Thad whipped her wristband up to check: it still shone turquoise. That was supposed to indicate their surroundings were safe and secure. "Maybe she hadda pee?" Thad rubbed her eyelids with the heels of her hands.

"Didn't see her anywhere on my patrol." Hadn't heard her either, or smelt her or sensed her in any way. Her skin felt suddenly cold.

"She shy. Don't hafta be no big deal if she went off lookin for privacy. Leave her be is likely our best plan." Thad stood up, belying her words.

"Can't you just—"

"Yeah yeah. Lemme home in on her, fine out what she up to." Fingers stroking shadows along her wristband, Thad went outside. Phin followed her. By the weak illumination of the plant-covered slopes sheltering them, she saw her husband's fast-dimming wristband change from turquoise to charcoal. The charcoal was threaded with a squiggle of bright pink.

"Hunh. This bit a Dr. Ops tellin me Doe went on up toward Unrest on her own." Thad plucked the curl of memory carbon free and swept it before her like a sparkler. "Yes it is. Also? She not alone."

～

Doe must have waded or swum. Or more likely floated off on rafted lander sections, like Phin and Thad ended up doing. Because the beach dissolved into marsh a little ways past their overnight site—just beyond the circumference of Phin's last patrolling pass. Dr. Ops had marked the marshy ground on the map he gave them, but without noting its lack of solid pathways. Which made sense if you weren't used to walking on an actual surface of an actual world.

There were some disadvantages to coming down to Amends under an AI's care. Phin felt certain the positives—bodies modified to wristband-integrated specs meant for emergency trustee deployment—outweighed that sort of negative.

The wristbands' beacons, for instance. They tracked Doe's beacon to the foot of a vine-draped bluff face, as the day's first blooms burst into multicolored light. "Heyyyy! Hey there, my honeys!" Their wife shot up from the rock where she'd been resting and waved her arms as if she'd been waiting for them, as if they might have missed spotting her. Or the two women with her.

According to Dr. Ops, trustees had been dying at disproportionately high rates here on Amends. So the plan was that they would approach clients under the guise of seasonal wanderers, aka Rogues. They were supposed to be setting up their temporary quarters on Unrest's outskirts. Supposed to be waiting till clients came to them there. They were not supposed to be rushing off and communing with clients haphazardly in the wild. Who knew what story Doe had told these two? Did it fit the cover they'd decided on?

The names she introduced them by were right, anyway. That was easy, though; they'd agreed to stick with their real ones. The older client's reaction to meeting them seemed off, somehow: her faint smile stayed the same size, but emptied itself of feeling, and her gaze lost its focus.

"Trill and Dola come here to learn about prettybirds," Doe explained. "Say they thinkin prettybirds is pretty smart. We was right about them things countin at us! Say they done it before—say it could be how prettybirds an people can communicate! They wanna study em more an figure out the way it works."

"So why come you studyin em here?" Thad asked. "Ain't none around I can see."

"This is their feeding ground. Their killing ground, I *should* say." Dola, the younger woman, waved at a pile of driftwood behind her—driftwood covered patchily with odd, crumpled—cloths? Skins? Abruptly the driftwood became bones, dismembered skeletons heaped along the bluff's base.

"Prettybirds is carnivores?" Thad leapt heroically to the rock's surface, a good deal higher than their raft. "What else you know about em?" She held out one hand, and Phin tossed her the braided hardwires, then looked for footholds and climbed up beside her.

"Omnivores, more likely. We put out a big basket of rose-toohip porridge for them. First there was only one group of five sampling it. They weren't eating lots—we thought we'd have to bring most of what we'd made back to Unrest. But once that group split, a whole flock showed up and cleaned our basket out. Took most of a morning."

Thad raised her eyebrows. "Really? Was you there the whole time? You could tell it wasn't some other animals?"

The older client, Trill, dropped her semblance of a smile. "What makes you think we don't know what we're doing?"

"Sorry!" Phin put her hands in her tunic's pockets and looked down. "Sorry," she repeated. The flat-topped rock was stippled with irregular streaks of a bluish, hair-like growth. She shuffled carefully to the edge nearest the bone piles.

"Why apologize? You're not the one who said any—"

"We both feelin it. Sorry, like my wife say. Lissen, we all three innerested in prettybirds too. What you know? Don't got em where we from."

"Where's that?"

A brief, awkward silence. "Up by Panonica, didn I say?" Doe answered.

Phin winced to herself. This was a serious change in their strategy—they were supposed to deflect questions like that: origins, why they'd gone rogue, what they wanted from the locals…. She turned her eyes to the sky, searching for something to distract the clients, and there— "Is that—what do we call it when they all fly together? A 'flock'?" She waved a hand at a stippling of darkness against the brightening dawn.

"Flock is one of our usual words, but Trill and I have started using a few special terms depending on the prettybirds' activities. We should come up with a name for those groups of four or five or six. They're common enough. Meanwhile—" Dola pulled open the woven bag slung crosswise from her sturdy shoulders and took out a complicated-looking instrument of wood and—could that be transparent plastic? Glass?

She held it to her face. Some sort of lotech visual prosthesis. Phin ran one finger over her left brow, then her right, repeating this trigger to her internal lenses till the individual components of the flock were revealed. Then she smoothed things back out so she would see it as a whole again. Glowing golden in a rare shaft of sunrise, they wheeled and swirled in patterns reminiscent of mud drifting up from underwater footsteps. Or rippling grasses stroked by the wind's many hands, or—

"When they do like that we call them a murmur, after the name of starling birds on Earth acting the same way." Dola lowered the contraption from her eyes and offered it to Phin. "Want to see?"

"Wait! Here comes another murmur! They might be about to mix!" Trill was talking fast and pointing. "We've watched this happen five mornings in a row now—before that they only did it once—twice if you count that time we came in the middle of things—"

Phin saw a second murmur coalescing over the mainland to the peninsula's south, seeming to detach itself from the low, dark smudge of the forested horizon. Larger and larger, nearer and nearer. Now both murmurs flew toward them. An arm curled around Phin's waist—Thad's arm, and she responded by pressing into it and reaching for Doe, wrapping a hand around her wife's wrist. In moments more the murmurs would converge—

And the two tightly spaced groups of prettybirds exploded in the air, loosened like unbraided hair to spring wide and high and so low they almost touched the waves. They expanded so swiftly, so hugely, that many hovered right in front of her, near enough that Phin felt the air move with the massed beating of their wings.

"How do they keep from crashing into each other? They aren't even facing all the same way!" Dola crouched to set down her bag, swapping the visual prosthesis for a tablet and stylus. She began scribbling furiously as the murmurs merged. The older woman, Trill, was shouting what sounded like nonsense:

165

"Scoo pups! Deedly-doo! Fiyah free Anna yogotta plizter!" Arcs of prettybirds knit living chains between the murmurs' different parts—or did they? Phin lost track of individual prettybirds in the billowing rainbows filling the sky. They fell in and out of focus as they darted up, over, and around one another, intricate patterns impossible to follow, overwhelming her eyes for what felt like hours.

And then the murmurs separated. The display was over; the prettybirds dispersed, flying in fives and sixes in all directions. A few flew above their heads, disappearing as they crested the bluff.

At Phin's feet, Dola was still marking up her tablet with alphanumerics, though less frantically. Trill leaned forward and blocked the view. "No, no—it was 'Fiyah free' *first, then* 'yogotta'!"

Thad tapped on Trill's upper arm. "Scuse me, but you wanna tell us what you talkin bout? What you doin?"

"Excuse *you!*" Trill shoved her face toward Thad's. "What makes you think you have any right to ask?"

"We're Jubilee's Prettybird Dopkwe," Dola explained, her voice a mixture of apology and boast. "We've been studying the prettybirds for over a year—almost two years. Right now we're looking at these periodic—um, we call them conferences. Which—"

"Which you would already have heard about—already *seen*—if you actually *did* come from anywhere around Panonica." Trill picked up the bag and held it open. "Come on, Dola. Pack it up and let's get home."

"You sayin we a lie?"

"Yeah. You're a lie. You're not from Panonica. How long've you been on Amends? Not long—six nights? Seven? You came down here straight from *Psyche Moth*."

"How you know that?"

"Apart from the way you pretend you're familiar with the tech advances we keep hidden from the last couple of trustees and Dr. Ops? And the way you claim prettybirds don't exist where you're from?" Closing the bag and grabbing Dola by the arm, Trill hopped off the rock's wide top.

"Mainly it's the fact that two of you were married to Wayna. My dead mother. Yeah. Who told my dad and my other mother your names, and a whole lot more. All about you guys."

Disaster. Cover blown. Phin's head hurt like she'd hit it hard. "Wait!" she shouted. Clenching fingers dug into her hip, Thad restraining her, preventing her from chasing their client contacts down. Or chasing them up; as she watched them walk away, the clients' backs, clad in dun-colored spun fibers, slowly rose along some half-concealed footpath climbing the bluff's steep, green-clad sides.

Alone, they sank to sit facing each other. The hair-like patches growing on the rock were softer than they looked. Thad spoke first: "Why, Doe? Why you run off an do like that?"

"You think we should just play things the way Dr. Ops wants us to?" Doe twisted to appeal to Phin. "Don't you think he might be wrong? About sumpn? At least a little?"

Phin wasn't sure how to stop the fight. "I—"

"Din you hear what the woman just said? Wayna *dead*. Ain't nothin bringin her back."

"I *get* it. I got it back when Dr. Ops told us himself, back when we was in orbit." Doe's words were for Thad, though she stayed turned toward Phin. "But what I *don't* get is what's the reason we aren't supposed to tell anybody who sent us and where we're from and why we're here."

Waiting. Waiting. As if Phin could explain what Dr. Ops meant. Thad had studied the rules the AI followed, studied them hard. But Phin was the one he had first fallen for. Phin was who Dr. Ops had explained himself to.

She attempted to put herself in his place. In the place of his wholeness, not the scattered sites of the purpose-limited fragments he'd given them. "Guess he thought it could contaminate the data we collect."

"If we tell the truth? Which people are gonna find out anyways—they ain't stupid!" Now Doe whipped her head around, away from Phin and Thad. Too late. The tears had already spilled from her eyes. Her shoulders vibrated with suppressed sobs. Phin felt her throat phlegm up in sympathy. She stretched one hand out to caress her wife's back.

"What?" Doe snarled, twitching away.

"You ain't even cried when we foun out Wayna died." Thad put her hand on Phin's hand to stop her from reaching out again. "I'ma ask you a second time: Why?"

"Okay." Wiping at her face with her shirt's short sleeves, Doe snuffed in a wet breath. "This is where she *lived*. When she lef us an come down onto Amends it was cause she wanted to be part of what was happenin here. What still happenin. An Dr. Ops part of what these clients tryna get rid of, an I just hafta tell em we his family. So maybe they gonna kick us out? That's they right! Or maybe they gonna realize we useful to em in some way, him too, and extend everybody some courtesy. Either way, this the best path to take. This the way we honor Wayna. This the way we oughta remember her."

"Well. You done?"

"Yeah." Doe laughed a short laugh. "I kinda went on and on a lil, din I? Sorry you asked?"

"No."

"Me neither," said Phin. "We need to understand." A breeze kicked up, coming in off the water. The bluff's vines swished against each other in the sudden quiet. "We need to understand. And now we do. I do. And I agree."

Another susurrus-filled pause. "Yeah. Awright, so what we do nex?" asked Thad. "Now we broke Dr. Ops' rules?"

"You know they wasn't rules. Just what he thought would help."

Phin stood up, loose blue "hairs" drifting off her in the light breeze. "Tell him what happened. See what he suggests."

➤

In addition to exploring Dr. Ops's parameters, Thad had the most experience with wave comms, though that had been in WestHem, back on Earth. She had been a pirate narrowcaster before her arrest. That was why they were supposed to get her to feed Dr. Ops their wristbands' findings and safely capture whatever updates he sent to his algorithms.

Escorted by a smattering of prettybirds — smaller than a flock but larger than the group who'd originally counted at them — they returned to stay another night at the Unrest outlier site, sleeping again in the abandoned house. No use setting up their lab here if they decided to move or go mobile after consulting Dr. Ops.

The prettybirds settled for the night on the house's roof and the crown of a stunted Hannakka bush nearby. Their jewel-like brightness dulled as the bush's illumination began fading. As Phin watched, they blinked in sequence again — the same sequence? She wanted to try counting, but where should she start? Arbitrarily picking a green-plumed individual perched on the house's overhanging eave, she recorded its two blinks on her wristband. Lucky choice, she thought; this was the way the first run had begun. But then things deviated. To that prettybird's right another gave her two blinks, too. And two blinks came from each of the other four prettybirds on the roof. The order didn't matter. It was all twos.

Switching to the Hannakka bush, Phin recorded the blinks of the five prettybirds there. Four each. A totally different sequence. What did it mean?

This time Phin took the middle watch, which in practice meant she stayed up sexing with Doe while Thad looped through the area around them like a nosy incel, stopping in occasionally but heading off before becoming too involved. Finally trading places with her was a relief.

Nothing noteworthy happened during Phin's watch. Toward the start of it Phin was sure she spotted *Psyche Moth's* steady light setting in the peninsula's south and west. Correctly calculating when and where it would reappear distracted her a short while. She could have used the calculator algorithm embedded in her wristband. Should have. If they ever met his whole self again — *when* they met his whole self again — Dr. Ops was going to know how much she missed him whether she had tracked his position with the calculator or not. He wouldn't have to read the wristband. He'd read her.

Denial did nobody any good. Too bad she couldn't just shed certain segments of her being. Though to be fair, Dr. Ops hadn't truly gotten rid of the segments of himself where his love for her lived. The algorithms he'd sent down here with them were only copies. Besides not being that broad. Still, Phin spent a long, wistful time wishing for conveniently detachable personality fragments. Or drugs, or some other way to forget she was part of a whole. A mere member of her family.

When Doe took over from her, Phin went inside to bed down with Thad, who hardly stirred as Phin snuggled her bedroll up to Thad's side. Shouldn't her husband be awake and worried? Wondering whether Doe would sneak off on her own again despite promises to the contrary? Planning what to tell Dr. Ops? And how? Frustrated by Thad's deep sleep, Phin rolled to the mat's far side and dropped into her own dreams.

She woke to curses. The house walls filtered most of what Thad was saying, but her shouts of "Fuck me! Fuck me limp and dry!" broke through. Doe occupied Thad's former spot on the mat, and Phin had snuggled close to her during the night. Cautiously, she inched out from under her wife's cradling arm and went to the house's entrance.

Drag marks creasing the side of the dune to Phin's right led up to the wave dish her husband had assembled from lander segments. Thad stood near the dish, fists pounding bent knees, silent mouth open wide, sucking in a big breath for more shouting. Phin scrambled forward and ran to hug her. "What's wrong? Stop! What if a client hears you?"

Thad unclenched her fists and stepped out of the hug, tugging off her wristband. "Here! Take it! Or throw it away—*he* don't care! *Forget* Dr. Ops! He don't want us comin back up, and he not comin down, neither." The stretchy carbon loop waggled on her fingertips. Streaks of apricot and baby blue marked active algorithms.

"What do you mean? You asked for us to be sent back to *Psyche Moth*? How? Why? There's not enough room for us to live there—not in the meat—"

"Think I'm stupid? Tole good ole Dr. Ops we'd give up our bodies." Thad had been suspicious of downloading ever since *Psyche Moth* arrived at Amends. Phin felt guilty for convincing her to try it. But this was too much.

"You can't say that! No I won't! You never asked if I would—or Doe, either, I bet—and besides, what's that got to do with our problems? Why even bring it—"

"So we could stay together, right?" Doe's new voice, reedier, higher, but carrying the same weight it always had. Phin's wife stood at the bottom of the dune's slope, looking somehow safe and comforting in her still-unfamiliar white body. "We family.

171

Les ack like it." Doe climbed up to them faster than Phin would have expected, gathering them both in her arms.

Thad stiffened, then relaxed. "Yeah, that's what I want. Yeah. Maybe…maybe that's what Dr. Ops is aimin at too? In his peculiar way? Cause his only family before us was his mama, WestHem. Who gave him birth by givin him part a her own self…." Thad's softened stance sank to a crouch. She pulled Doe down to squat beside her. Phin joined them. "An ain't that kinda what he gave us fore he landed us here on Amends?"

"You squirted him the playback from your wristband?" Doe asked.

Thad nodded, absentmindedly squeezing her wristband, scrunching it together in the palm of her hand. "Includin what I copied off yours and Phin's. Then I ast him what to do now summa these clients figured out who we really is, where we really from. An he answer me like everything already fixed up fine—like he *been* here! Like Trill an Dola already took us under their wing an sponsored us, an we already plugged in to Jubilee an Unrest an everthing! Like them pieces a himself he give us is all its gonna take, and he ain't hafta do nothin more!"

"What exactly he did he say? Not what you decided he meant. Did you make a recording?"

"Wanna hear it?" Thad lifted wrist and band to her mouth without waiting for a reply. With an exaggerated slurping sound she licked at a glowing speck of neon green, then smiled and spoke Dr. Ops' words in her own voice:

"'At this moment, you have almost all of me you need. You can solve your clients' difficulties instantly—yours too. As soon as you realize these prettybirds aren't a new problem but an old solution, you'll figure out exactly what to do!'"

"That's it?"

"They's more, but nothin to do with nothin."

"Because he wants us to figure things out for ourselves. He's the complete opposite of what that trustee who met your wife—"

"An died right after, remember?"

"—what that trustee, that Carpenter Marie, claimed clients said they hated about Dr. Ops: him making everybody's decisions for them, keeping everybody dependent. He's not like that!" Phin thrust out her chin as if she could force acceptance of her opinion.

"*We* know. We *know* that—firsthand. We on a whole world thinkin otherwise, though."

"Gotta show em."

"Show em what?" Doe rotated her arm back and forth so her wristband twirled in place. She slid it off and let it dangle from one finger. "Show em how we—"

SWOOP! A blur of pink and blue snatched the band away. "Hey!" Doe's yell scared the thieving prettybird off—but not far. Phin saw it land on the roof of the abandoned house below them, alongside others. Four others? Had the prettybirds who'd perched there last night stayed the whole time? As she watched, the thief dropped the wristband and blinked at her twice. Slowly. Deliberately. A pause heartbeats long and two more blinks.

In unison with its companions.

Would the prettybirds repeat themselves? Concentrating on the rooftop contingent, Phin almost missed the second steal: a different prettybird was flying off with Thad's wristband clutched beneath its amber and violet belly.

She jumped to her feet. "Stop it! Drop it! You! Stop!"

"What?" Thad noticed her hand was empty. "Wait—what's goin on?"

This prettybird went straight to the scrubby little Hannakka bush. It hung the wristband on the branch where it perched and blinked at her four times. Pause. Four more times. And yes, the others with it did the same.

"Don't know for sure. But I think—" Phin tugged off her own wristband and ran down the dune to place it on the sand at the slope's bottom. She ran back up and continued, "—I think they're talking to us. Or actually it's more like they're getting us to understand how to talk to them."

"We spozed to blink, that it?" asked Doe. She stood too, now. "Together?"

"No. Not quite— Yes! Here we go!" Over the treetops massed beyond the dunes came a murmur of prettybirds: black specks diving, swirling, wheeling through the air, a vast cloud quickly covering their sky, sinking low to fill her sight with color upon color, wine and rose and ivory, teal and mauve and all the spectrum, all the glories, all the shades and all the light. Hovering within reach.

Like a stream of rain, the cloud released a line of twittering prettybirds. Five of them. They dropped to the ground and formed a semicircle behind the wristband, facing Phin and Doe and Thad.

They blinked in unison. Eight times.

Phin waited patiently.

Eight times more. Her theory was correct! She kissed her husband hard, reached for her wife and kissed her too. "I'm right! I'm right!" She laughed for joy.

"*Now* we blink?"

"You want them to think we're like the wristbands? That we're algorithms, tasks, like the dedicated pieces of himself Dr. Ops sent down with us? Look! They're taking them in, parts to the whole." She pointed. The three groups of visiting prettybirds had taken off. Beneath the airborne belly of one prettybird in every group hung a wristband. In an instant the individual prettybirds merged into the murmur.

"What they gonna do with Dr. Ops's algorithms?" asked Thad. "Cain't download em I bet."

"Not these. Although—" She gazed measuringly at the throbbing mass of hues blending, bending, shaping, changing, reaching, bringing its outside in and its inside out. Touching itself. "—although maybe I'm amazed how quickly it's managing to adapt."

"Yeah? You think they gettin the trick a—"

"Not 'they.' 'It.' Single prettybirds aren't intelligent. Not on their own. It's—"

Doe gasped. "The murmur! It's like a family—like us!"

Phin frowned. "Not like us: like him. It's not a family; it's the equivalent of Dr. Ops."

"You mean—you tellin us you got a theory…" Thad gestured at the murmur's kaleidoscopic churn. "…tellin us prettybirds built themselves a AI?"

"I'm telling you they made themselves *into* an AI."

"Natural artificial intelligence?"

Phin remembered Dr. Ops telling her back on *Psyche Moth*, so long ago, that all intelligence was artificial. Or natural. Or both.

And he was her love. More. Her heart, like they all were. And he was right. "The only kind there is."

Publication Histories

"Introduction: My Recipe for Making Amends" first appeared in the *MdW Atlas* in August 2022.

"The Best Friend We Never Had" first appeared in *Apex Magazine* in June 2018.

"Over a Long Time Ago" first appeared at *Lightspeed Magazine* in May 2024.

"Living Proof" first appeared in the anthology *Mother of Invention* in September 2018.

"Out of the Black," originally titled "Deep End" first appeared in the anthology *So Long Been Dreaming* in September 2004.

"Like the Deadly Hands" first appeared in *Analog Magazine* in December 2016.

"In Colors Everywhere" first appeared in the anthology *The Other Half of the Sky* in April 2013.

"The Mighty Phin" first appeared in the anthology *Cyber World* in November 2016.

About the Author

Nisi Shawl is best known for fiction dealing with gender, race, and colonialism, including the 2016 Nebula finalist novel *Everfair*, an alternate history of the Congo. Its sequel, *Kinning*, was released in 2024. Shawl is also widely known as the coauthor, with Cynthia Ward, of the Aqueduct Press Conversation Piece *Writing the Other: A Practical Approach*. With Dr. Rebecca Holden, Shawl co-edited Aqueduct Press's anthology *Strange Matings: Science Fiction, Feminism, African American Voices, and Octavia E. Butler*. They are a cofounder of the Carl Brandon Society, a nonprofit organization dedicated to improving the presence of people of color in the fantastic genres, and they've served on Clarion West's board of directors for two decades.

Filter House, Shawl's first Aqueduct Press story collection, co-won the 2008 Otherwise/James Tiptree, Jr. Award. *Our Fruiting Bodies*, a collection of more horror-oriented stories, is their most recent Aqueduct Press title before this one.

Shawl edited the World Fantasy, Locus, and Ignyte award-winning anthology *New Suns: Speculative Fiction by People of Color*, published in 2019 and *New Suns 2*, published in 2023. Additional awards include the Kate Wilhelm Solstice Award and the British Fantasy Award. Shawl lives in Seattle, one block away from a beautiful, dangerous lake full of currents and millionaires.

Printed in Great Britain
by Amazon

57271509R00108